"These stories by Kathy Fish and Robert Vaughan are rich, textured, and physical – they smart with tension and possibility. RIFT is peppered with appealing, complex characters and atmospheric details."– **Megan Mayhew Bergman**, author of *Almost Famous Women* (Scribner, 2015)

"You can shave with the razor-like fictions in this collection from Kathy Fish and Robert Vaughan. These stories are as sharp as they cut deep, very like the people featured here, who come up and square off against each other in these dangerous, domestic arenas." – **Robert Lopez**, author of *Kamby Bolongo Mean River* (Dzanc Books, 2009)

"When Robert Vaughan and Kathy Fish, both masters of the form, combine forces, the end result is nothing short of breathtaking." – **Michael J. Seidlinger**, author of *The Strangest* (OR Books, 2015)

"Reading Fish's and Vaughan's electric collection is like listening to two seasoned singers trading songs in a tunnel: their voices echo, resonate, and harmonize in impossible octaves. Rift is a book of sublime melodies that sustain and remain." – **Ryan Ridge**, author of *American Homes* (University of Michigan Press, 2015)

"I have been a devoted reader of Kathy Fish's stories for years. Countless times, I have turned to her work for instruction and comfort. And if possible, this collaboration with Robert Vaughan, Rift, has strengthened my devotion. The stories here are full of precision and heartbreak. This book is an accomplishment, elegant and sparse, and richly imagined, and I loved it." – **Jensen Beach**, author of *Swallowed by the Cold* (Graywolf Press, 2016)

"These stories made me not sit still. They turned me around and turned me around." – **xTx**, author of *Today I am a Book* (CCM, 2015)

"Vaughan and Fish are twin aficionados of flash. Side by side, in RIFT, they captain language catching great tunas (of memory), so this book sails as fleet. Vaughan as name means "little" (he's BIG) and Fish can be "tuna" (prize fish)! The Little Tuna are a specie that rush and dart, reaching speeds of 47 miles an hour (fact)! These flashes are far faster, sleeker, and sharper than that–physical enough to hold gasping in hand." – **Luke Goebel**, author of *Fourteen Stories and None of Them Are Yours* (Fiction Collective Two, 2014)

RIFT

stories by

Kathy Fish +

Robert Vaughan

FAULT ~ 9

TREMOR ~ *59*

Robert

What Lies Ahead
The Farms of Ohio Were Replaced
By Shopping Malls
Life After Love
What's Left Unsaid
Fling ~ Fatigue ~ Rejection
Philadelphia Cream Cheese
When He Left It All to Me
Help I'm Alive
Pets: Three Vignettes

Kathy

Birth of the Giant Sand Babe
The Blue of Milk
No Time For Prairie Dog Town
Abandon All Thoughts
Endangered ~ Out of Place ~
A Botched Affair
A Pirate or a Cowboy
Neal Figgens
Hello
Love Train ~ Lifelike ~ Spill

Kathy

Tool
Peacock
Grip
Pulse
The Four O'Clock Bird
Sea Creatures of Indiana
River
Go Dog
The Possibility of Bears

Robert

Postcards of a Life
Dew Drop Inn
Dehydration
The Literary Savant
Keep It Curt
Four Stone Cups
Picnic
Cosmos at Aspen
No Face World Champ

CATACYLSYM ~ *163*

Robert

Me and You and a Voice Named Boo
Adrift
Too Much Oxygen
The Tangerine Ibis
Loose Canon
A Box
The Guy in This Sky
No Soul
Dream Maker

Kathy

Everything's Shitty at Price King
A Rift, A Stampede
Come Loose and Fly Away
Strings
Swell
Collection Day
A Proper Party
This is How Eventually the
World Falls Apart
Akimbo

FAULT

A break in the continuity of a body of rock or of a vein, with dislocation along the plane of the fracture.

A Room With Many Small Beds

1

I am eight years old and this is the year I learn to float. My father's girlfriend, Pearl, tells me to stay in the car. I lean out the window, watch her climb steps and pound on someone's front door. A man comes out and stands with his arms crossed. She rifles through her purse, pulls out a dollar and holds it in front of his face. Flicking her lighter, she sets it on fire. All three of us watch it burn.

2

Bobby Kennedy has been shot. It's two o'clock in the afternoon and we have not eaten. Pearl sits cross-legged in front of the television with her cigarettes and her nail file. Her hair is set in empty frozen orange juice cans. She looks like a space alien or a sea creature. The neighbor kid is standing on our front lawn. I ask him what he wants. *Get the lady*, he says. Pearl goes to the screen door. *Has the new baby been born?* she asks. The kid hops from foot to foot like he has to go to the bathroom. I tug on Pearl's shirt. *His mother's dead*, I whisper.

3

I sit under the elm tree in our front yard with a jar of moths in my lap. I have forgotten to punch holes in the lid like my father told me to and now the moths are dead. I want to float away, but the sky feels like a giant's hand, pushing me down. I open the jar and eat them, one by one.

4

Mary has risen to heaven. She is wrapped in blue. Angels hold a golden crown above her head. I'm staring at "The Coronation of the Blessed Mother" in my 4th grade Bible. We're supposed to be memorizing the Five Glorious Mysteries, but I can't stop touching her cheek with my fingertip. Sister William is screaming and the kids are laughing, but I'm with Mary, suspended in clouds.

5

Pearl's on the phone with her sister, saying *Yes, but* and *Maybe you should* and *Don't*. When she hangs up, she says her sister is high. High means she's going crazy again. High means she won't stop talking and that she'll probably get in her car and drive to Florida and the police will have to go find her. Pearl gives me bean with bacon soup and a glass of milk. She asks me what my problem is. She asks me how I know the things I know. Her arm slides across the table like a tentacle. She pinches my face.

6

My father's laughter wakes me. I look out my window. He and Pearl are lying on a blanket in the back yard. He strokes her long, blonde hair. I imagine Pearl's hair feels like moonlight. She unbuttons her blouse. I watch and grow cold. Lately, I've been getting into trouble for not paying attention. At school. At home. Pearl tells me if my mother were here she'd spank me. *No she wouldn't,* I say. *She'd spank you.*

7

Alone, I practice leaving my body, drifting to the cobwebs on the ceiling. From there, I see everything. I follow the rush of leaves off the elm tree to Pearl and the man on the sidewalk below. I see her take his hand for just a moment, then let go.

8

We wander the halls of a mental hospital. Pearl tells me I was born here, back when it was St. Francis. *Why are you crying, baby?* she asks. She gives me a hanky that smells like roses. I'm hot inside the boxy wool coat I've been ordered to grow into. We're looking for the Vance twins. They had been Pearl's playmates. She tells me they are Mongoloids so I think they're from China. A man in striped pajamas hooks his paw around my neck and pulls me into his room. He clamps his hand over my mouth. I feel myself rising like steam from a pot. I see the man on top of me. I see my skinny legs kicking, my knee socks puddled around

13

my ankles. Pearl runs into the room and jumps on the man's back. I see her biting his ear and I am happy.

9

Pearl slides lipstick over her mouth and grabs the keys. She's wearing her fake fur collar and fake fur-trimmed ankle boots. Johnny Mathis is singing "It's A Marshmallow World" and the record's skipping on *marshmallow, marshmallow, marshmallow. We haven't had dinner*, I tell her. My feet stick out of footed pajamas that Pearl has cut the feet off of. She kisses the top of my head. I know she's going back to the man, to the house where she burned the money. My father and I will never see her again.

10

In my dream, our house has fifty-foot ceilings, a steep, spiral staircase, and wings connected by tunnels like the Pentagon. My father oversees the installation of an intercom system. He wears a whistle around his neck like a P.E. teacher. My mother is with us. She has never left. I discover an attic room with many small beds, but there are no children to sleep in them.

Galloping into the Future

1

I sat, flask out, in a bar in Gallup during a thunderstorm. From the covered patio of the Horse Hair Diner adjacent you could smell charcoaled flesh being served to hungry bale-throwing hands. My stomach growled, but I only had money for either booze or food; not both.

2

It was then I barely noticed her, standing, all alone in the rain, in front of the Brassiere and Lingerie shop and Cheese establishment. Her hands held a cloth, a flimsy billowing scarf to her face and she appeared to be crying. Was it the storm, or a lover? A death she'd discovered?

3

I was swept up by the strings of the Hungarian gypsies playing down a side street, and for a split second I felt transported back to Paris, after an unsuccessful evening at a brothel, perhaps the uber-elegant Chabonais, where I'd crossed paths with an ever-zealous Edward VII on late summer nights.

4

There were eyes, the ladies in the window of the diner staring around me, smoking. And hers, there in the rain, without moving, her shoulders breathing slightly. Getting wet. It was as if I was in their movie, and they, in mine. I ordered another whiskey to see what other liquids the evening might have in store.

5

The music came to an abrupt halt. I heard galloping footsteps outside the diner, what sounded like hundreds of cavalry pummeling the hard packed earth. I noticed several other patrons moved their hands swiftly to their guns. I began searching for an exit toward the back of the bar, and she stood there, motioning me.

6

In a leap, I bolted toward her as shots rang out, and shouting began. She whisked me upstairs, her hand as delicate as a chickadee inside mine. We entered a room on the third floor, and she ran to the window, attempting to open it. "It's stuck," she whispered.

7

I forced it open, and she smiled, nodded me to follow her out onto the roof. There were people all over the town who were watching the events unfold below. "What happened?"

I asked, and noticed my tongue was thick, and I was more inebriated than I'd thought.

8

She lay on the roof, staring up into the darkening sky. "See that?" She pointed. "It's Leo, just there by the Big Dipper." The bullets whizzed past us, and the fighting continued as we hunkered down. "Someday I want to live there." She turned toward me, her lips moist, and we stared into each other's faces like statues.

9

Nothing is permanent, of course, I know. I was only in Gallup to avoid getting soaked. Never thought I'd end up there with this vision, on a rooftop, avoiding the town plunder, and feeling romantic. Never thought I would meet someone so quickly, squashed on that roof like a bug in a grill.

10

At first I wasn't sure it was me. We'd drifted off, entwined, her in my arms, breathing in unison. The guns continued to roar, but you could barely hear the blasts. Something startled me awake, and she was gone. I bolted up, was it all a dream? No, there was her scarf, fluttering against the wood shingles.

Düsseldorf

I have not left the room in three days and the maids are impatient to clean it. It's October and my husband has brought me along on his business trip. We've been to London and Paris. Now we are in Düsseldorf and the sun never shines. I keep the drapes closed, order room service, nibble Kuchen under the eiderdown. The room smells like rotten apples.

There's an art museum somewhere. I could take a cab or walk to the museum or I could lunch by the river. According to the map in the guidebook we are not far from the river.

In Paris, in a smoky brasserie, my husband spoke all through our calf's head dinner about his client. He said she is smarter than any man and young, but wise and savvy.

"I hate the word savvy," I said, and swallowed. "And all women are smarter than men. It is no great accomplishment."

When he talks to her on the phone, his voice changes register, as if he's been told he's won a major prize. I wonder what she looks like.

The maids pound on the door again. I go into the bathroom and lock the door. I can hear the rattling of keys, their stout, German voices.

The bathroom doorknob turns back and forth. I wait for them to give up and leave me in peace.

"Frau? Frau?"

There's nothing to it. I open the door, smiling, grab my sweater and my bag with the guidebook and an umbrella and leave them to the clutter.

There are no people on the street. It's Tuesday, the middle of the day. I walk a long ways. I turn corners and stop, forgetting which direction I came from. Nothing looks as it ought to. The gray and brown buildings stretch to the clouds.

I find a bench and flip through the guidebook. I don't recognize anything from the pictures. All the streets appear the same. Only chestnut trees. Only plain, boxy buildings. Maybe I should return to my hotel. Lying on the grass, not two feet away, there is a dead squirrel.

A little boy in wire-rimmed glasses comes towards me. He's eating a sandwich wrapped in foil. I ask him if he speaks English.

"Yes. I speak English," he says, around the bread and cheese.

"Good. Can you tell me where we are?"

He laughs and says, "This is the city of Düsseldorf." He offers me the rest of his sandwich. I decline.

"But where are all the people? Where are the birds? I haven't heard a single bird chirp or dog bark. Where are the cars, the streets signs? If this is a city, where are the shops, the cafes, the restaurants, the bars? Where did you get that sandwich? Who makes the music and the art? Where are all the feral cats?"

The boy chews his sandwich and swallows.

I sniff the air. "Why, I can't even smell anything, can you?"

"Düsseldorf is a beautiful German city on the Rhine River. Its population is 11 million," he says.

"I don't believe you."

The boy crumples the foil into a ball and throws it at my face. He tears off down the sidewalk.

Maybe the squirrel is only sleeping, but I've never seen a squirrel sleeping out in the open. It seems a risky thing for a squirrel to do.

Early in our marriage, my husband brought home a rescue dog. A Border Collie mix. We named him Rex. He mostly sat in the corner of the laundry room, chewing his paws. Gradually, Rex came to trust us and we took him everywhere. He slept between us, licked our faces until we woke up. One day he simply disappeared.

The guidebook says that Düsseldorf is a city known for its fashion. If I can find a shop, I'll buy my husband a tie. I'll buy him a hundred ties in every color and drape them over our bed. I walk the streets for miles but there are no shops and no ties. For one crazy moment, I imagine Rex bounding towards me, like there you are, I've been looking all over for you!

Over the tops of the buildings, the moon rises. I am alone and Düsseldorf is empty. I stand in the middle of the street with my arms raised, calling my husband's name. And it keeps coming back to me, over and over, like a verse.

Time for Dessert

The couple sits on their front porch every summer night. Although the view remains the same, they never tire of it. The steady river birches in the side yard. A martin's house across the road. Darting swallows chatter, catching multitudes of bugs.

He says, "Warmer this evening." Sucks down the last bit of his third Manhattan, nibbles the cherry.

She nods, pulls the sleeves down on her cashmere sweater. Can't seem to ever get warm enough. She points. "Look at how huge that ship is."

"They usually don't let barges like that on the St. Lawrence."

It's the main reason they moved to such a remote location. He loves water, boats, and all the activities associated with them. That, and he'd also burned through most of their friends before retirement age. One too many drunken spats. They sit and watch boats motor by. A bee buzzes on the roses near the screened door.

"Are you ready for dessert?" she asks. "Fresh peach pie."

"Yup."

She ambles inside and he stares at her rocker's motion, hypnotized. He sets it to an old favorite melody, Ella's "Let's Call the Whole Thing Off". From the kitchen he hears the familiar sound of plates clinking, the microwave beeps. He sees a fancy motorboat toting a teenaged skier. His mouth waters.

Tomorrow, he thinks, I'm going to get up early and go fishing.

All by myself.

Vocabulary

He scratched my back from neck to tailbone. Curling, looping, like handwriting. I was his paper. It made me shiver. Out his window, I glimpsed a bloated moon. He had me lie on a towel that felt rough, as if it had dried on a line. We didn't say much. Earlier, he'd frowned, lifting his eyes from his phone. Asked if he knew me. I said, *You don't and you won't.* That was in the coffee place, in the strip mall near my work. A whole vocabulary ago. That was in the morning.

If You Have to Have an Ism

She twirls her cell phone end to end. She's waiting for someone to never arrive. Stands there smirking with her border-lined hoodie and her sellout sadsack song and dance. Flip, flip. This is a lady who never got a break. This is a woman scourging the day, the snow, the *the*. Flip, flip. This is a person, goddamnit, not a woman. It's a person who wishes she was an individual.

Bear

The place in Keystone was a dump. They had a gift shop on the first floor. I wanted a souvenir.
I twirled a rack holding rabbit's foot keychains.
Disgusting, you said.
Cruel, I said.
The shopkeeper said, *Fake*.
But I could feel the reedy bones under its fur.

I tried on butterfly necklaces in gold, blue, and green.
Gaudy, you said.
Folksy, I said,
The shopkeeper said, *50% off*.
But I didn't see any price tags.

We climbed some rickety stairs to a room filled with electric stars and moons, beanbag chairs and flutes. A large bear carved from a tree. You could get pot there. They had brownies and a special oil.

We'll take two of everything, you said.

I want the bear, I said.

The shopkeeper said, *Not for sale.*

But I knew exactly where I wanted to put it.

She Wears Me Like A Coat

The first time it was one of those cucumbers wrapped in plastic. I stuck it down my pants when no one was looking. We floated through the store, my heart beating a million times a minute. I kissed her in the check-out line, world spinning away, some actress's boob job gone wrong. I wondered what might happen if I got a cucumber hard-on.

We never said a word about it once we got home. We lived with another tool, one of her friends from college. Slade was always there. I'd suggest studying at the library, or checking out a band at the Nugget. He was cemented to the kitchen nook.

Later that night we're out looking for astronauts, and she said isn't it a little too late for this. We sat under the picnic table, shared a cig, the smoke lit her turned-up nose pink.

"That was stupid," she said.

I nodded, it was the cucumber. "Yeah."

"What? It's not like we can't afford it."

"It isn't about that."

She punched my arm. "Everybody knows you never, NEVER EVER lift from a store you frequent."

She was our shopper. "I don't frequent them. You do."

"Look, you want to do this, fine. But spend some gas, drive to Dover. It's a town filled with lifters, grifters, and swindlers."

I mulled it over, ground out the cigarette.

That night, after she drifted off, I lay awake. It wasn't the small stuff I was concerned with. Twinkies, or gummi worms. I had grander goals. My neighbor's chainsaw. Our babysitter's scooter. Finally, I fell asleep imagining a world in which everything was mine, anything I wanted came instantly. Rooms of senseless stuff. And for this, I would get severely punished. Yes, old school style.

There Is No Albuquerque

I was born with three physical defects, noted in my chart, noted also in the Baby's First Year keepsake book my mother had received as a shower gift. She wrote down the date and time of birth, my weight and length, and this, the one and only entry:

Crossed, pale eyes, a hole in the neck, three bumps on the forehead of unknown etiology and without apparent pathology. Named her Betsy.

My kindergarten photograph: I'm wearing thick glasses. The hole in my neck is now only a small indentation. The bumps on my forehead have grown into horns, clearly visible through my bangs, like three raised fists.

Soon after that photo was taken, my parents died in an elevator crash and I was placed in the care of a distant uncle, a clown named Buddy. He gave me the name, "Dinosaur Girl," and put me to work as a sideshow freak. I was kept in a pen and tethered to a post with a rope around my neck. Pregnant women and the weak of heart were warned to steer clear, but for twenty-five cents anybody else could stand in line to pat my head and stroke my horns. They were said to bring good luck.

Thanks to a series of online courses, I have secured work as an indexer and an abstractor for the psychological association in a building downtown. I work in a cubicle surrounded by stacks of books. My coworkers do not talk to me. My boss, Mr. Kenton, however, talks to me all the time. He likes hearing about my freak show days.

I tell him:

When I was little, my mother used to stand me before the mirror every morning and make me say: I am beautiful. After she died, I kept doing it for a while until Buddy told me to stop. After he married the Tattooed Lady, they soon lost interest in me, and I was sent to a foster home. My foster parents thought I was retarded. They told everyone who would listen that they saved me from a dumpster. I ran away when I was sixteen.

Mr. Kenton appears to love all of humanity. It is his only flaw. Mr. Kenton is dashing. The kind of man who would look good in a hat. I wear a bulletproof vest under a very large shirt. I resemble a turtle. But I am safe.

The itching drives me crazy. Sometimes I go into the break room and scratch the spaces between my horns with a pair of tongs. The same tongs we indexers and abstractors use to pull pizzas from the toaster oven. Do not tell anyone.

The plastic surgeon says if he were to remove the horns I'd go blind. *Guess I'll hold on to them*, I tell him.

Mr. Kenton calls a stand-up meeting in the middle of the day. This is unprecedented. He announces that he has been promoted and is taking a position in Albuquerque. He is leaving in two weeks. Some of the women start to sob. Janice goes right up to him and hugs him with everyone watching.

(Many animals go through a season of molting, shedding their feathers, fur, shells. Some even lose their horns. When will be my season?)

On some particularly fine days, if the lines had been long, Buddy would let me sit on a stool off-stage when he performed at night under the Big Top. I was allowed to eat all the Sno-Cones I wanted.

Never once do Mr. Kenton's eyes flick up to the bumps on my forehead. That takes some restraint. I admire him for it.

I tell him:

Once a farmer from the adjoining county came to the fair and paid his quarter to pet my horns. He'd waited in the hot sun for a long time, eventually removing his shirt and tying it around his neck to staunch the sweat. When his turn came, he approached me and drew a gun from his pocket and aimed it at my chest, crying, Beast! Beast! One of the carnies threw himself at the farmer, who dropped the gun. After he recovered his breath and his senses, the farmer put his shirt back on and walked away. No charges were filed.

As soon as one is upright, the soft front of the body is exposed and vulnerable. One must brace oneself for onslaught.

I had rushed out one morning to get Mr. Kenton breakfast. He'd worked through the night and sat slumped in his desk. Crossing the street, I dropped the styrofoam container and it sprung open. Some of the food spilled on the pavement and I scooped it up with my bare hands before the light changed.

When he opened the container and stuck his plastic fork into the omelet, I could no longer keep it in. *Don't eat it! I dropped it on the street!*

Mr. Kenton examined the omelet and said, *It looks okay to me.* He ate every bite.

There is no one like Mr. Kenton.

I like to plan adventures that involve wearing a helmet large enough to accommodate my horns. For instance, I have a scuba diving lesson next week. I have learned to operate a Jet Ski.

I am planning a skydiving adventure surprise with Mr. Kenton.

When Janice comes into the office still wearing her bike shorts and her bike helmet, I say, *Yeah*! And raise my hand for a high five as she walks past. She must not see though because she doesn't high five me back.

Buddy emails me sometimes. He writes, *Dear Dinosaur Girl, (haha).* He says clowning is a young man's game. Some freaks lost their livelihoods when society turned its nose up on the shows. *I was only trying to help*, he says.

He wants me to know I can visit him anytime.

This Friday, Mr. Kenton and I will leap simultaneously from an airplane, high above the clouds. There is no promotion and there is no Albuquerque. We will hold each other's hands as we plummet. Our parachutes will bloom like jellyfish and we will hush and slow, falling softly to the earth. I am beautiful.

The Rooms We Rented

1. *Palm Springs*: Her tucked hair peaks out from behind both ears like detangled detours. The skintight dress she wears, not a dress, maybe a shift, has lines like the LA freeways, and a red sun appliquéd on the center of her chest. She is an undelivered Christmas cactus in the searing desert.

> *What we learned: We knew so little about the outside world, had no radio and no TV. And that woman never taught anyone anything worthwhile.*

2. *Bangor, Maine*: On the days she went to church, she braided her hair to her right side so she could see her split ends with alacrity. In between rounds, she'd ask herself: Am I breathing underwater?

> *How we changed: She now spoke with just a trace of transatlantic lisp—in a voice that had*

nothing whatsoever to do with who she was or
where she came from.

3. *Madwilly, Tennessee*: Today the detainees who usually sit at hidden cubicles are paraded around like a Silicon Valley start-up. They call it points, and I call it farts in a tight space, with no air that collapses your hormones while you wait, alone, in your blind, with your hairline follicles afloat.

> *Our mantra: 'All I want to do is come a little*
> *closer.' Lifted from the port-o-potty wall.*

4. *Houston*: Before she left for overseas, that last night, she told me, all I dream lately is how to get you underneath me. And by underneath, I mean the ocean floor.

We Learned to Pronounce Prokofiev

The music teacher always arrived after morning prayers. Sister Constanza would announce her, stuff her used hankie into the bib of her habit, and march out. Before Mrs. London, music class had always been just singing songs from the songbook, like "Faith of Our Fathers" and "The Battle Hymn of The Republic." I never minded. It felt like recess.

Mrs. London had honey-colored hair, all poofed up and falling over her shoulders. She wore short dresses and make-up. Our 5th grade classroom was in a garret, with its own staircase and restrooms in the old, old building where my father and his father before that went to school.

I loved her frosted lipstick smile. She put records on for us to listen to. She played *Peter and The Wolf* and taught us that the bird was a flute, the duck was an oboe, the wolf was a French horn. Peter was all the stringed instruments. She taught us that music could tell a story. We learned to pronounce Prokofiev. *He is Russian*, she said, *and he made this music for you.*

Mrs. London taught us to identify the instruments by sound. She taught us that a piano was in fact a percussion instrument. I wanted to learn to play piano but knew the answer before I asked: We can't afford it. So I got a book from the library and pretended for a while, but what good is knowing the notes if you can't hear the music?

One day Mrs. London came back to our classroom to retrieve a forgotten record and she found me in the cloakroom reading *Valley of the Dolls*. She said, *Does Sister know you're in here?* I told her no, tried to hide the book behind my back.

That's a good one, Mrs. London said. *But maybe you should read something meant for young girls.* She held out her hand and walked me back to my desk, past Sister Constanza, who was leaning back in her chair with her mouth hanging open.

We listened to *Peer Gynt*. She played "Morning Mood" and asked us if the music had sounded familiar. We loved how "In the Hall of the Mountain King" made us feel, that slow, steady beat that got faster and faster. We used it when we jump-roped,

40

going, *da da da da da da da da da, da da da, da da da,*, speeding up until we collapsed on the playground.

Mrs. London smelled like flowers and air and snow. I wanted to smell like that. I wanted to not have my hair in tangles, pulled into a rough ponytail that made me look like a horse. When Sister Constanza screamed at the kids, I'd study the long crack on the ceiling. It stretched like an arm and splintered into fingers. I imagined the ceiling was the floor and I was standing on it, a wide expanse of pure white with a hand coming out, like someone buried alive.

I followed Mrs. London once. She lived near me, in a beautiful old home of pink brick and lacy white ironwork. I thought I would ask her to teach me piano after school and I would do chores or help her correct papers in return. She seemed to glide more than walk. But a man was there, Mr. London I guess, and he kissed her for a long time. I saw him slide his hand inside her sweater. I stayed and watched for too long, then turned and ran home.

In January, at the end of class, she announced she was going to have a baby and that the school no longer wanted her to teach music. She said she needed to start preparing to be a mother, but that we should keep listening to music and learn to play whatever instruments we wanted. She walked up and down the aisles, stopping to touch my hair.

Last Exit From Liberty

In a town the size of Liberty, the news spreads faster than an airborne virus. Just leave, she thought, follow your intuition.

She paced up and down the black and white kitchen floor. She wondered if they'd tapped her telephone.

The wind gusted, the limbs of a maple tree scraped against her roof.

She grabbed her cell phone, took three deep breaths, and dialed her sister in Montana.

"I'm coming for a visit," Cora told Madge. She peeked through a corner of the kitchen curtains. The police were still parked outside. And some news van with its station's logo on the side.

"You're what?" Madge asked, her nasal tone grating.

"Driving out, leaving tonight." Cora glanced in the hall mirror, noticed the two dark circles under her eyes. She walked toward the bedroom, intending to lie down. Instead she stood in the doorway, stared at the bed.

"Oh." Madge paused. "Are you sure you can leave, so...so-"

"I'm sure," Cora nodded. "Yes, I have to get away." She sat on the living room sofa, counted the bills from a tan envelope in her purse.

"But, why so sudden?" Madge asked. "Are you in trouble again?"

It was the way she said *again*. "No, it's not me," Cora said. Two hundred dollars. That ought to be enough. She tucked the envelope back into her purse.

"Is it Mitch?" Madge asked. "He didn't hit you again, did he?"

"No." Cora fell silent. *Should I tell her?* Everyone else in Liberty knew. And it was better coming from her twin sister than some tacky news story.

"He was arrested, Madge."

"Arrested?" Madge said. "ARRESTED? Oh, heavens to Betsy."

"Yeah," Cora said. "It sucks."

"What was it this time? DUI?" Madge guessed. "Or did he beat somebody up at Barbers?"

Cora closed her eyes. "It's porn." And that was way less than half of it. What she wouldn't tell her sister was the rest: It was kiddie porn. Mitch, in the leading role.

She dropped the phone, rushed to the bathroom, hand over her mouth.

The phone dangled over the edge of the sofa.

Woe

Plants. Neurobiology journals spilling over coffee tables. Work tables. Beakers with odd contents. One large black & white poster of an austere looking man. Photos of twins and triplets, children and adults, old people. Rotten tangerines in a bowl. I tell him I was an identical twin. *The other was lost in utero*, I add, as I try to clear a space for him. He watches my hands, the left one curled permanently as if holding a baseball. *I was born this way*, I tell him. (Too much woe, too soon. I should shut the fuck up.) He opens the drawer where I keep the corkscrew. *You're okay*, he says. It's as if we have been here before. In this room. With this winsome cat. He says, *All this science I don't understand.* I feel our future unfurling before us. I know exactly how the air will feel on the patio. I remember rain on a clear night. I know the sound the back door will make, the squeak of its hinges, when he finally leaves me.

Night Life

You know all the cool places to go. The darkly lit hell-holes with languorous types. Boys with money to piss away and looks to kill. Girls with degrees in the art of bullshitting. They make short attempts to communicate with you as if there is some future there. You want to tell them not to bother. You learned the hard way how to trust silence.

You used to pretend you couldn't speak English but lately that doesn't work. The city is infiltrated with too many bi- and tri-linguals. They're everywhere: grocery stores, gas stations, even your neighbors.

Move your head stiffly, feels like you slept on concrete last night. Haven't done that since you left New York City. Talk about shitholes. Some girl who thinks she is a woman smiles at you from the corner of the bar. She drinks Corona-with-a-lime-thank-you and her boyfriend is the geeky type who thinks because of her he's really hip. He's got a ticket to ride.

You could go back across the street to Formosa. It's a little darker there. A little more serious drinking

47

crowd. Last time you were there some drunk English guy wouldn't leave you alone. He kept instigating differences of opinion on vague topics and then insisting he was right. As if there is no other way. Like the death penalty or British authors. Who can argue about these things?

An actor/dancer whose face resembles Clark Kent on a bad day sits down opposite you. "Mind if I sit here?"

You can't even answer a simple yes or no question. You feel the need to brush your teeth. Say: I suppose so.

Clark is scoping out the scene. His head moves like targets on an artillery range. So, what is this place anyhow?

Suddenly you've become the expert on nightlife trivia. You say anything you want it to be.

Clark smiles at you in an intrigued way. It makes you feel nauseous. Could be the Cabernet. I'm just visiting L.A. and some waiter told me this place is cool.

You nod vaguely. You know you're supposed to say oh yeah? Where are you from? Or what waiter told you or what is your idea of cool? Instead some voice in your head is saying fuck this. Over and over.

Enigma

I let a stranger buy me a French toast breakfast. My train had been delayed and I was hungry and had an earache. I'd spent all my paycheck on the ticket. When we sat down, he took off his hat and I said, *Please put that back on.* Without the hat, he looked like a toe. He drank coffee while I ate. *What's in your locket,* he asked. *A memory,* I said, trying to sound enigmatic and over eighteen. I rubbed my ear with my knuckle, asked for more. The locket was empty. I'd found it earlier in the ladies room.

~

My aunt said she'd take me with her to Australia if I agreed to dress like a man. She got me a boy's suit from the Salvation Army. A couple of puffy jogging suits. A fedora, a baseball cap, and a haircut. *I'm sorry, but this is the world we live in,* she said. *I do not wish to be preyed upon.* My aunt had orange hair and crooked-ly drawn eyebrows. She wore lots of jewels. Our first night in Sydney we went to a pub and a man punched me in the face.

In Spain, they let you stay for free in the nice resorts if you're willing to spend a few hours every day talking to businessmen who want to learn English. You do your time then you get to hang out in the spa or the pool. I broke the rules and let one of the men buy me a drink. Something like sangria with 7-Up. He asked me how he was doing. *What is inside your—necklace? Locket*, I said. *It's a locket.* I leaned across the table and flicked it open.

Temporary

I like temp jobs. But there's something repulsive about getting close to people—office parties, cakes for babies about to be delivered—I'm not cut out for the long haul. I like cubicles with partitions so I can pick at my teeth, yawning when I've been up the previous night until two in the morning watching re-runs of *The Twilight Zone*.

Secretaries ask me, "How many days?" Their voices are edged with envy, like they'd love to know when the monotony will end. It's a question between prisoners behind bars, confined within the drab walls of a 12-Step Meeting.

When I was at the law firm last year, Mickie, one of the paralegals, told me I'd make a good candidate for the bar. I told her it depended upon whether the bar served Ketel One. She bellowed, and I saw every tooth in her horsy mouth, and beyond: throat, epiglottis. I could have been swallowed by it. These companies do that: and then spit you out.

I worked picking flowers in the towns around Humboldt County: Arcata, Eureka, Forestville. I had to watch a video about picking safely, equipment handling, in a room with three Mexican men. The video had no Spanish subtitles and they looked wary, waiting for the images to somehow translate enough of the story. I realized that this was the story of their lives, and mine, too. How much more did I comprehend any of it than they did? How much less?

I was a marching band coordinator in Pembroke, New York. A flautist told me all pianists were notoriously control freaks. I had no idea there was any kind of pecking order among ensemble members when I helped to market for the Santa Fe Chamber Orchestra.

I've worked sales and marketing jobs where I'd tell strangers, "You're going to love this gel!" or "Imagine how you'd feel wearing that Chronograph." I offered money-back guarantees, two for one bargains. There were dialogue scripts that I'd tweak, changing the word "FANTASTIC" to BRILLIANT or "PRETTY" to ENGAGING!

I've sold jewelry to the Japanese, catheters to cardiologists in Daytona Beach, butterfly nets to Science & Nature stores.

Once in between temp jobs in New York City, I volunteered at a soup kitchen for battered homeless women. My sister said, "That's horrible! How can you expose yourself to these victims?" Years later, divorced from her first husband, she quickly married the man who plowed their driveway. He had HIV. I said, "How can you expose yourself to that illness?"

During a heated discussion, a former girlfriend once retorted, "Why don't you get a real job?" It wasn't the first time I'd heard this. I didn't tell her that the thought of doing one job, any one task for more than a few months made me crazy. I didn't tell her that I felt the same way about girlfriends.

I changed the subject. "Did you know that we spend a third of our lives sleeping?"

She waited, accustomed to my peculiarities.

I added, "I don't want to sleep through the other two-thirds."

"You're just a big scaredy-cat," she teased. "Commitment phobe."

Girlfriends were forever pressing to hear the L word, to move in, to exchange rings, or vows. Most nights, I'd lie awake wondering why the exchange of body fluids wasn't enough.

Then another place would beckon: San Diego, where I could sell surfboards, or run the front desk at the Angola Inn in northern Minnesota. Or put out fires in Angel's Rest State Park, Utah.

Game Show

Mom and I are on her sun porch watching a documentary about a man who won lots of money on a game show by memorizing patterns. This morning she smells of the lavender from her neck pillow that's supposed to be for travel, but she wears it all the time now. In the mornings I have to remove the tape she's put on her eyelids. She claims this keeps them from drooping. She tells me to grab an edge and just rip, like a band-aid, so I do and her shoulders jump but she doesn't make a sound. *How do they look,* she asks, and I say, *Red*. I've made her pumpernickel toast with lots of butter, and coffee the way she likes it, extra weak. After the show we go to the rec center to swim laps. I complain about the chlorine bleaching my hair, so she buys me a swim cap with daisies all over it. She swims one lap, rolls onto her back. Her belly sticks up like a bright green island. I swim back and forth for several minutes until my mind goes nice and numb. I dog paddle over and tread water next to her. *That man was trying to cheat the system,* she says. To my mind he was just smart. When I was in middle school, she and my dad sent me to a psychologist who gave me an I.Q. test. I scored 142. He said my behavior problems were due to being bored at school. I don't remember being bored. I spent a lot of time in the principal's office playing cards with the assistant. Now I manage a beauty salon downtown. I don't even know how to cut hair, but I can schedule people, take appointments, make sure the money all adds up at the end of the day. Mom starts hacking and I tow her to the edge. She thinks she has lung cancer. I think it's just post-nasal drip and paranoia. She's survived four bad marriages and a year of homelessness. She tells me surviving's not enough though. I know what she's getting at. The game show guy eventually lost all his winnings on a Ponzi scheme. The IRS was after him for back taxes. He absconded to Florida, became a Buddhist, and died in a car accident at forty-nine.

Figurines

Today my mother broke every dish in the house. The Lladro Three Wisemen were the first to go. I didn't mind, in fact, I even helped her trash those Asian figurines that loomed on the former glass shelf unit in our living room. She'd bought them when she took a Feng Shui extension program at the local college.

The whole thing took less than an hour, and when we'd finished, Mom said, "Fuck your father, let's get in the Explorer and drive to Florida."

My sister was starting to decoupage ashtrays out of ceramic plate fragments. "Don't do that, Frieda," I said. "You might cut yourself."

Before we'd reached the interstate, Frieda fell asleep. In the quiet twilight, I thought about the Wisemen, broken dishes, shards of rubbish. Just before leaving the house, I'd snatched a Fu Dog head, stuffed it in my coat pocket for protection. Now I rubbed its head, feeling the jagged edges at its neck where it broke.

TREMOR

A relatively minor seismic shaking or vibrating movement. Tremors often precede larger earthquakes or volcanic eruptions.

What Lies Ahead

We were taking turns at the wheel, and our breaks were getting less frequent because we wanted to reach Jefferson City before sunset and the prairie was making me ill the way it looms before you like the promise of a job but never delivers, and I realize I don't want to grapple with this now so I suggest Tony close his eyes, hands at ten and two on the steering wheel, to see how long he can keep the car in a straight line without veering off onto some lopsided course and the casserole Tony's mom made us that we've eaten for the past three days would come spewing up from deep within and just before my hope soars in thinking what lies ahead of us in Jefferson City, in that shithole of a burg without soul, it overwhelms me how I can be this lonesome sitting beside my best friend who I'd saved from drowning when we were kids goofing around on the Platte River and as I look over at him, eyes still closed, I see my future there, like these tumbleweeds he somehow magically misses as they spin off across the plains.

Birth of the Giant Sand Babe

The three of us drive straight through from Cañon City to Laguna Beach so that Zach can see the ocean for his birthday. All we have to eat are these sample bags of Snap Pea Crisps Zach scored from his job at 7-Eleven. He quit that job on the spot, scooped up the bags, filled the tank of his rusted Dodge Caravan and off we went.

Eighteen hours later we arrive, unclean and hungry. Zach has eaten all of the Snap Pea Crisps, claiming they tasted like those styrofoam packaging peanuts. Rick and I will never know. But hey, now we're here and it's hot and blue and beautiful. Zach's running into the surf, pulling off his shirt.

The little children in their goggles and water wings are right to eye him suspiciously.

Later he and Rick decide to encase me in wet sand as I lie motionless, staring up at the puffy clouds. Thanks to them, I am now endowed with very large breasts and a sand wig cascading outward from the top of my head.

Encased and cool. Like being in a sensory deprivation chamber. Like William Hurt in that movie. Maybe I'll start to hallucinate. Bring it on.

It's hard to be at one with nature because Zach won't shut up about the Siamese twins he saw at 7-Eleven back when he was still working there.

We don't use that term anymore, Zach, I tell him, watching his hand pass over me with a clump of sand meant to even out my breasts.

What?

We say "conjoined" now.

Okay whatever. They came in, these conjoined girls with their dad, wanting Slurpees. Slurpees!

Quenching one's thirst is a universal human imperative, Zach.

I know, but Siamese twins!

Them too.

Rick says, *Where were they connected?*

Every once in a while he hovers his face over mine and asks me how I'm doing. The sand's packed tight around my ears. The ocean's muffled for me. Their voices, blessedly, too. But Rick really wants to know.

Oh this is the best part, Zach tells him. *They were joined at the head.*

Probably why they were still joined, I say. *Too risky to separate them.* My voice sounds weird to me, like it's coming directly from my brain.

I fade away. Close my eyes. Relax deeply, feeling the warm sun on my face.

Oh crap. Could you guys put some sunscreen on my nose?

Rick's sweeping dabs of coconut smelling lotion across the bridge of my nose and I'm thinking, never stop.

I sneeze, shifting tectonic plates. Chunks of my sand self break away.

Shit. Sorry guys, I mumble as they put me back to-gether. I close my eyes again. Muffled music. Chil-dren. My own breath. The dogged heartbeat of the ocean.

This totally rocks, Zach says for the one hundredth time. He loses interest in burying me and runs away. I guess into the surf again. I no longer feel Rick work-ing on me either. I fall asleep in earnest, enter a dream world where Rick is kissing me, slowly unbuttoning my blouse, only his fingers are sausages.

Guys, I was thinking...

Zach again. Water dripping on my face. I smell actual sausages grilling nearby.

Are there Siamese...?

Zach, goddamn it. Conjoined.

Right. Are there conjoined triplets? Because that would rule. They'd be like a human vine.

Neither Rick nor I respond to this.

Would you like out of there? he asks me.

I believe I would.

They dig enough away from me until I can move my arms and legs again. I lift my head and sit up. They are both grinning at me. My best friends. What else do I need?

If we had a camera I'd film this close up and in slow mo. I'd call it "Birth of The Giant Sand Babe," Zach says, wistfully.

A sand babe. I like it, Are you having a good birthday, Zach? I ask.

The best.

Then Rick takes my hand and pulls me to my feet and kisses my sandy lips, just like that. It's a perfect, gritty kiss. It is perhaps the most glorious kiss ever.

The Farms of Ohio Were Replaced
by Shopping Malls

We were on a bus trip to Cuyahoga Falls. Long story short I fell into an online gambling club that was tracing the lyrical references in Chrissie Hynde lyrics. Two people boarded the bus in Vegas, and highjacked us, one held the driver at gunpoint and told him to drive straight toward Wyoming. Or Idaho. The other rallied us all into the last four seats, three side-by-side (there were only twelve of us) and told us that her name was Rhea, named by her momma after a moon of Saturn. Told us all of the kids in her family were: Titan, Enceladus, Dione, Mimas (who died in childbirth). I could tell she was lying, the way her eyes were slits, the sides of her mouth curled up like the Grinch. She kept staring at the dragonfly tattoo I had on my neck. Brenda, who was in the middle between Vern and me, smelled like she'd just eaten guacamole. Her leg kept jittering like a spring outburst of rain. Just then we heard singing and the woman highjacker shouted, "Lover of endless disappointments with your old collection of postcards, I'm coming! I'm coming." And we all clapped, as if it was a line from the latest play on Broadway. She kept her eyes tightly shut and I recall thinking, any one of us could snitch her handgun. But I already knew, what has been fated cannot be avoided. I slunk further down in my seat, wondered if I would ever get to see Cuyahoga Falls in this lifetime. Or the next.

The Blue of Milk

There was a woman who went to the park at night and swung on the swings and drank from a bottle in a paper bag. When she became dizzy she would stand and remove her clothes and walk the perimeter of the park singing low.

There was a man who walked his dog, who saw her, but kept to the other side of the street and never entered the park. When the moon was out and shining she looked blue he thought a naked blue or silver or the blue of milk but he tried not to stare.

There was a small child who lay in bed waiting for his mother to return. He decided one night to follow her.

The man saw the boy trailing far behind the woman. The boy dragged a blanket. The man surmised this must be the woman's child. The man kept to the other side of the street and didn't enter the park.

All the nights after this were the same with the woman taking off all her clothes and circling the park and drinking from the bottle in the bag and the boy trailing behind like a ghost and the man walking his dog and seeing them both but keeping to the other side of the street and not entering the park or calling out to the woman and the boy.

The nights grew colder. The woman persisted with taking off her clothes and the boy persisted with following her in just his thin pajamas and the man persisted in walking his dog but the man began wearing a coat and the dog, too, wore a coat that matched the man's.

One night the man's dog, a terrier who was getting old and blind, started to bark at the woman as she passed by and the woman and the boy, trailing behind her, were startled and for the first time noticed the man and his dog and the woman stopped and the boy stopped and the woman cried out and the terrier strained at his leash and the man felt now he had no choice but to cross the street and enter the park and apologize for his dog and get the woman to put on her clothes and maybe help her and her son back to their house and god knows what else but now he probably had to do something as they had both seen him.

The terrier stopped barking and the man bent to pick him up as he crossed the street and entered the park and approached the woman who was crying and patting the head of the boy whose arms were wrapped around her naked legs.

The man said I apologize if my dog frightened you I don't know what got into him but see he's very sweet really and you can pet him if you'd like. The man knelt and the boy reached out his hand to let the terrier smell it. Both the boy and the woman petted the terrier and let him lick their hands and the man tried not to look at the woman.

Ma'am he said you seem to have misplaced your clothes can I help you find them? The boy looked up to his mother now embarrassed but the mother only said yes let's find my clothes and she set down the bag with the bottle in it in such a way that it would not tip over.

Her clothes lay on the ground near the swings and the woman pulled them on. They were only pajamas and it had gotten quite cold now and the man took off his coat and put it over the woman's shoulders and his stocking cap he put on the boy's head and now everybody looked quite normal and it seemed okay to walk them home which he offered to do.

It turned out that the woman and the boy lived not far from where the man lived, on his own with the terrier, though he'd never seen them during the day or any other place in the neighborhood. She asked him to come inside and she would make them all tea but she was unsteady on her feet. She said this is our abode and it sounded like a warble and she made a sweeping gesture with her arm and the boy started to cry. She went to the kitchen and the man sat down with his terrier on his lap and the boy lay on the floor with the blanket knotted in his fist.

The woman brought a cup of water with a tea bag in it but the water had not been heated. The man watched the brown color of the tea swirl slowly into the clear water and said I would like to help you if I can do you need some money or food do you have a job what can I do? The woman said there is nothing to be done or said we are fine you finish your tea and go please.

The boy dragged his blanket to the other room and the woman said we need to sleep now and she came to the man with the terrier on his lap and gave him a kiss on the cheek. The man could see her breast through the opening in her pajamas and he touched it and mouthed it and she let him and she liked it and this is how they were for some time, her bent to the man, the long strands of her hair falling onto the little dog's head and over his blind eyes, in the quiet of the woman's abode.

Life After Love

The ceiling fan whirled, manic, creaking way too fast. For a moment I pondered what might happen if it came off its hinges, randomly beheading the various other occupants of the waiting room. Might be fun.

I glanced over at Mom. Her eyes were closed, perspiration rested lightly on her forehead, just above her glistening painted-on eyebrows. And above her lips. Was their air conditioner broken? I'd never get used to the Florida humidity. I'd arrived only two weeks earlier, when Dad called and said, "You'd better come...now."

I scanned the room for the a.c. unit, saw one way back toward the corner near the toy basket. Near the bald kid, about five, playing with the Bert hand puppet. I shuddered, wondering how many other kids had put their hands up that same toy. I wiped my hands on my shorts.

The couple across from me kept staring. I thought Mom's wig might be askew. She was so fastidious about her looks. Well, she had been. As usual, we'd argued that morning about which one she'd wear with today's muumuu.

"I like the black hair better," I'd said, trying it on next to her in front of her bureau. It was long, Cher reborn, in those Sonny and Cher, I Got You Babe, days. "It makes your blue eyes pop."

"Pop?" She'd said, like any word was an effort to get out. "That wig is too strange. The hair gets caught in everything. No, I'll wear the short blonde one."

Ugh. She looked like a shih tzu. Or Ethel Mertz. The black one suited her better. Now, sitting there, I thought of Mom as Cher, with her hair streaming out behind her, singing, "Do you believe in life after love, after love, after love..."

No Time for Prairie Dog Town

Sam sees the sign for Prairie Dog Town outside
Oakley, Kansas and wants to go. *Go, go, go*, he says,
pointing to the huge, fake prairie dog by the side of
the road. His new haircut is lopsided, making his
head appear misshapen. Sam has a way of not looking
you in the eye but making you feel stared at just the
same.

He came along with me because he said he didn't
want me to be lonesome. Being lonesome, for Sam, is
the worst possible thing. And I didn't trust myself to
make the twelve hour drive alone on no sleep. Sam
works as a custodian/cleaner in my building where I
work writing advertising copy. I've known him ever
since I moved to Colorado. One night when I was
working late, I saw him pushing a vacuum around,
gravely studying the carpet. We started talking. Or
rather, I started talking. He gave me a Snickers bar.
Besides my boyfriend, he may be my best and only
friend.

I'm trying to get home to Iowa before my brother dies. My phone chimes with regular texts on his condition. I texted my oldest brother: *Anything I can bring?* He texts back: *Food.* So I've got a casserole on ice in the cooler, hamburger, noodles and corn, drowning in cream of mushroom soup. Iowans love shit like that. Three dozen chocolate chip cookies. A fifth of Maker's Mark. Sam's munching on Fritos and now the whole car smells like corn. My belly churns.

Sam, buddy, get me a pop. He reaches back and pulls a Dr. Pepper out of the cooler and opens it for me. All I know about Sam is that he's 28, lives with his mother, and never finished school because he hated "spesh ed."

When Sam says my name, he draws it out slow. *Loooooorie. Looooorie.* He's kind of singing it now. Kansas is an awful state to drive through. I feel my eyes start to glaze over. But Sam can't help with the driving. I'll stretch my legs, maybe vomit in the grass at Prairie Dog Town. Let Sam have some fun.

Nobody in my family knows I'm pregnant with my boyfriend's child.

Looorie. Loooorie.

Hey bud, can we just listen to the radio? A new text: *Morphine only now. Hurry.*

Sam's twisted around, digging in the cooler. Rumble of ice cubes. Frito crumbs embedded in the spaces between his teeth when he smiles at me. I pull over, get out of the car, and puke in the grass.

My boyfriend says we're not ready for a family or marriage. He's probably right. After we got the call, that my brother was on his way out, I curled up in his arms, said I needed something life affirming. Like a baby.

We'll get a puppy, he said. *We'll read to cancer patients, plant a Japanese maple in the front yard, maybe try cliff diving.*

The last phone call I had with my brother I said how unfair it was that he had MS and what a shitty, mean disease it was. He said he was at peace with dying.

Are you still with that guy? he asked.

Yeah.

That's too bad.

We both laughed.

Sam gets out of the car. He's wearing his Members Only jacket. He's so damn proud of it. Seeing my vomit on the grass makes him cry for some reason.

We move away from the puddle and I slip off my clogs. It's early spring and the ground feels pleasantly hard and cold. Cars whiz by. Kansas stinks. I may have to puke all the way to Iowa.

Sam has found an antler. He holds it aloft like a sword, shouts to an invisible foe, *Beware!*

I love you, Sam.

Sitting close, he rubs my back. *Looorie, Looorie,* staring somewhere past my shoulder. *Sore,* he says. *Sore.*

There's no time for Prairie Dog Town, Sam. I'm sorry.

He points. I turn and see a gray and white hawk winging upwards. It's huge. My cell phone chimes and I curl my hand around it tight. I tug on Sam's jacket, pull him down. We lie on our backs and watch.

What's Left Unsaid

He turned the car off, exhausted. The drive had seemed endless, hours elongated like taffy. He stretched his arms behind his head, challenged his burning eyes to stay open. In the distance, he could see the wisp rising from their sugarhouse chimney. He figured she'd be up already. A crack of dawn slipped through pillowed clouds, more dark than light. He loped toward the house, opened the kitchen door, set his bags down.

As he crossed the pasture, Serena whinnied inside the barn. She always sensed when he was close. He paused under a maple, looked down at his calfskin Tony Lamas. Wondered how he might explain blowing all their retirement savings in Vegas. Maybe he could work more overtime, save up again. Then he wouldn't have to tell her.

Abandon All Thoughts

One afternoon in January, when all seems lost, a man coils himself up inside the braided rug in the foyer of his home. For the first time today, he feels safe. It reminds him of how the nurses taught him and his wife to swaddle their babies, for comfort. Tight, tight. Babies are frightened of their own bodies. Unused to the freedom of movement. It's like a new womb.

Outside, the cottony sound of the neighbor man calling his dog. Mumble of a garbage truck moving up the street. Warmth penetrates his very bones. His limbs relax. The only thing uncomfortable is his breath, ricocheting back into his face. He wishes he'd flossed this morning. He wishes he'd thought to remove his clothes. He will meditate here for a while, possibly forever.

Audrey Hepburn, the cat, leaps atop the rug and starts pawing and scratching until she grows bored and runs off to find a patch of sunlight to lie in.

His son comes home from school. Cursing, he nearly trips over the rolled rug. He circles it a couple of times. Jumps up and down on it.

"Ouch."

"Dad? What are you doing?"

"I don't know."

Silence.

"Um. Okay. I'm going sledding with James. Bye."

His daughter comes home, too. She is a cheerleader.

"Pete texted me. He said you were acting cray."

"Leave me alone."

"Can I bring you something?"

He says no, but she returns. A straw scratches down the front of his nose.

"Take a sip."

"I'm afraid I might choke."

He hears her climb the stairs to her room. Overhead, her backpack thunks to the floor.

His wife comes home, waking him.

"What's all this?" she asks. Lila must have texted her.

"I lost my job."

She kneels before the opening of the rug and pats the top of his head. His crown chakra.

"It'll be okay. We can live on my paycheck. We'll just have to scrimp until you get back on your feet. Darling. Unroll thyself."

She wanted to be an anthropologist but now she works as a substitute teacher. He thinks of how her face must look right now, rippled with concern. She left the house this morning wearing a fleece sweatshirt with bright yellow bees and the words "Bee Kind" on it.

Now here she is, peering into the rug and touching him. It's not sex. It's not even affection. But it's something.

The man shifts his weight, attempting to roll. Eventually he gains momentum. Something loosens. The rug unfurls. He finds himself lying on his back, breathing the cinnamon and cat pee smell of his home. He opens his eyes.

Fling ~ Fatigue ~ Rejection

Fling

"Poor little me," she mused. She is dripping with sweat while the rain spits bullets. She feels like flinging coffee at the Pope. What could be worse than an abortion in a Boston alley, the doctor a stranger. The father stranger still.

Fatigue

The coffee didn't help. His fatigue was bottomless, so much that as he fell asleep at the wheel, barreling through the balustrades of the Golden Gate Bridge, not even the barometric plunge would wake him up.

Rejection

They listened to Everything But the Girl in her tiny

room tucked beneath the staircase. When he tried to kiss her, she ran to the bathroom to throw up. Alone in her room he prayed aloud before he swallowed the entire bottle of Nembutal.

Endangered ~ Out of Place ~ A Botched Affair

Endangered

I meet my boyfriend at the usual restaurant. It's cold outside, but the place feels toasty. I shrug off my coat and pick up the menu. He's reading his phone.

"Oh no," he says. "Saolas are on the newly endangered list."

One of the few things I know for sure about him: Saolas are his favorite animal. They live in the rainforest. They're like unicorns, which are also endangered.

We've been dating for three months.

"You ok? You seem a little off," he says. "I bet I can make you smile."

I take a sip of my water, suck on an ice cube. I've been thinking of taking a job in another state.

"Just hungry. I had to drive around a protest to get here."

"Really? What are they protesting?"

I can't think how he doesn't know.

He orders a burger. He tells the waitress he loves Colorado because he's a climber. She seems impressed.

"What do you think?" she asks me.

My boyfriend and I end our days wrapped around each other. He doesn't know I get up after he's fallen asleep and just wander our rooms in the dark.

Out of Place

We've just taken off from Denver and my ears start to pop. The engines sound like chainsaws. Chainsaws make me think of Texas, but I'm flying to Boston.

I unwrap a lemon drop.

"It gets better once we get above the clouds," my seatmate says. "Less turbulence." A businessman, he has all the comforts: a neck pillow, noise canceling headphones, special slippers. He seems out of place here in steerage.

He waves an open bag of Oreos my way. I shake my head. My stomach feels wobbly. I have an interview later.

Earlier, I saw people boarding a plane to Dallas. I haven't been home in so long. Boston's new. I haven't fucked anything up there yet.

The businessman goes on and on about what kind of plane this is. The features. I don't mind. I can tell it makes him feel good.

A Botched Affair

On particular kinds of nights I'll watch the Zapruder film on repeat. The slow motion one of the motorcade in Dallas that shows the exact moment JFK's head exploded. That burst of red. No matter how many times I see it, I wince.

My new boyfriend suggests a day in the park. Kites. Ham sandwiches. He buys me a black lab puppy. We name him Sprout.

One YouTube leads to another. Conspiracy theories. Alien abductions.

My boyfriend gets me special glasses to wear at night. Blue light from screens is my problem. But maybe I just don't fit the mold.

JFK's autopsy was a botched affair. They put a 21-year-old intern in charge of removing what was left of his brain. I spoon Ben & Jerry's into my mouth as I read.

One night over burgers, my boyfriend slips an emerald ring on my finger. The band is a metal I can't identify, coiled like a rope. It belonged to his grandmother. "I like old things," I tell him. "They remind me of ghosts."

Philadelphia Cream Cheese

I was born in the city of brotherly love. So they got me because deer are hopeful in more ways than one. They got me when I scored a goal. They got me by having bad taste and taking it from the boss. They got me when my roller skates collided with a lunch pail. But what matters is that every wing of the house is filled with feathers. Such a piece of a puzzle is this! I woke past noon. I am honey, I am several winds, my nerves wither. I don't love you.

No, I don't love you, brother.

A Pirate or a Cowboy

I find him sleeping in front of a fan, his shirt unbuttoned, a highball glass of Alka-Seltzer in his hand. The fan's blowing the little hairs on his chest over the scar that runs like a ladder from the button of his Bermuda shorts to his breastbone. The TV's on, playing *Silverado*, a movie he watches continuously. Ike, his dog, struggles to his feet and comes and licks my hand.

"Dad," I say.

He snorts awake, drops the glass on the carpet. The Alka-Seltzer fizzes anew. He sees the six-pack in my hand, the bag from The Wishbone in the other, says, "Oh hell yes."

We sit on the garden swing out back, drinking our beers and eating our tenderloins. His cheeks are greasy. I hand him a napkin. He's got a tattoo of a lightning bolt on his bicep and a gold tooth that shines when he smiles. He'd make a great pirate I think, even now, even as an old guy with a bad heart. A pirate or a cowboy.

We bend and straighten our legs, rocking the swing slow, watching a squirrel eat the ear of corn my dad's nailed to the tree. For some reason I imagine my dad's heart nailed there too. Given a supply of oxygen, the human heart can run on its own source of electricity and will continue to beat outside the body. But not, I suppose, with a nail driven through it.

"Kind of gruesome," I say.

"Yeah."

"You don't know what I'm talking about."

"Doesn't matter. Everything's gruesome. Even the *word* gruesome."

We sip our beers. I give the rest of my sandwich to Ike and crumple up the wrappers and stuff them into the Wishbone bag. Having cleaned the cob of kernels, the squirrel skitters up into the tree, leaping, leaping, leaping from branch to branch.

"Do you remember when you used to play the oboe?" Dad says.

"Of course I do." I have never played the oboe. I'm not even exactly sure what an oboe is.

He's fallen asleep again. His skin looks gray in the dusky light. I tap his leg and he opens his eyes.

"Dad I gotta go."

Ike shuffles ahead of us. It takes a long time to get from the swing to the door. We hear the surging music from *Silverado* playing inside the house. It sounds like victory, like triumph.

When He Left It all to Me

He had to leave, he said, though we'd met only days prior, and like with any men breaking boundaries we'd lain together despite barbed wire fences, pools with fathomless bottoms.

The morning he split, he thrust his blue down coat into my arms, said I won't need this, but it was a bitter day, when months later, that December, I found the tape in its pocket.

Eva Cassidy sang "Fields of Gold" and I can't forgive her for dying so young.

Where did you go?

Still can't listen to more than the first half; no, less than a quarter of that song.

Neal Figgens

A tall, skinny boy enters the pediatrician's office wearing a Poison t-shirt, jeans, and a fisherman's cap, pulled low over his eyes. He drops into a seat and the back of it bangs against the wall, startling a little girl.

She says, "You should probably sit over there," pointing to the portion of the waiting room reserved for the unwell. A picture on the wall shows a droopy-eyed child with a thermometer in his mouth.

The boy says, "hmm," and begins rifling through a copy of *Modern Parent*. He's thinking about a boy named Phil.

The girl walks over and stands in front of him. She's rubbing a satin pillow against her cheek. Her left eye is covered with a yellow patch with a smiley face on it. The boy hears a humming sound and doesn't realize at first it's coming from her.

He closes the magazine. "What I have isn't catching. Besides, I'm just picking up my mom."

"Very well," the girl says and returns to her seat. Her mother, sitting next to her, has not looked up from her book.

The girl sits swinging her legs for a bit, then jumps up and looks out the window. "Is that your truck?" It's an old 4 by 4, green, with "Midnight Dream Lover" stenciled on the side. An accordioned right fender.

"That would be my truck, yes. That's very distracting by the way," he says, pointing to his eye.

The girl touches her patch. "It's meant to be."

The receptionist hangs up the phone. "Neal, your mom has a couple more patients. I let her know you were here."

The girl, whose eye is drawn to the front desk, shifts her gaze back and forth from a poster on the wall behind the receptionist and the boy.

"That's you," she says.

Finally the girl's mother looks up from her book, to the poster, to Neal. He rubs the frayed edges of his fisherman's cap between his thumb and forefinger. The mother regards his toenails, poking out of his sandals. They are magenta colored and in need of a trim.

The poster shows a senior picture of the boy. He's sitting under a tree holding a guitar, managing to look both earnest and irritated. The particular name of his disease is written in block letters, as is his name: NEAL FIGGENS. The fundraiser was the receptionist's idea. She made the poster with markers and glue and glitter pens.

The boy says, "The deal is you can purchase a chocolate bar or you can purchase a bracelet that says 'hope' on it. Most people get the chocolate, but it tastes like tofu."

The girl jumps off her seat again. "Do you get all the money?" Her other eye, the one without a patch, darts around as if seeking its mate.

"The money goes toward my medical bills," the boy says. The mother turns the pages of her book, appearing not to read them.

"How does it feel?" the girl asks.

"Beth."

Upon hearing her mother's voice the girl starts humming again.

In Biotech, the teacher teamed him with Phil for the drosophila project. Three times a week, they stand side by side in the lab, breeding fruit flies in jars. Phil's lower lip is much fuller than his upper lip. The boy would like to bite it. He closes his eyes and feels himself sinking through the floor. As if to the bottom of a snowy ocean. It's happened before and it's not terrible, but he never gets used to it. Alarmed, he opens his eyes again.

"This helps," the girl says. She hands him her pillow. The boy presses it to his cheek.

"It smells good. It smells like lavender if lavender were very lonely."

His mother is a phlebotomist. It used to mean nothing to her, drawing blood all day long. Now there are days when she swears she can smell it and it terrifies her. Soon she'll emerge with her lab coat slung over one arm and she'll touch his cheeks with small, careful hands and he'll ask her about the veins. If it's been a good day, she'll smile and say the veins were great, as fat as earthworms.

"Do you fish?" the girl asks.

A woman walks in with a baby on her hip. She rocks back and forth as she signs in and the baby swings round, its eyes growing wide. The baby looks substantive and wise like a future emperor. Neal Figgens thinks he would like to hold this baby for maybe a minute. He watches the baby suck on its pacifier. The motion reminds him of a small, beating heart.

Help, I'm Alive

We called him the Blue Mouse at first, until we'd done it so much it simply became Blumau. Then Blau. He was scrappy, especially when cornered, would fight his way out of any ambush. And he had range, could outpace anyone on overnight raids to targets far off in the desert. Mostly he was stealthy, silent. Never talked. It was as if he moved behind a Plexiglas wall, preserved for only him.

I had no idea he would become my lover. He was already polar suns, all moons, endless creaking winds. Long sleepless nights I'd lie in my cot, think surely God was some relation. Turns out Blau was from the streets of Vegas. No parents, lived with a gang since he was ten. I found this out from Chunk, a dude who ended up AWOL in Paki. Slowly information trickled in from various guys in diverse places, like a game of telephone. Blau was completely unaffected. Shrugs, sideways grins, heading off to shoot rounds with Trey or Killer.

I'd lie awake at night wondering if he could hear my heart hammer. Hard to be soft, tough to be tender.

The next May day the rain pelted and the sky shuddered, pools collected in our fresh footprints. We pitched camp under a swarm of giant palms. It was that wet night, the first time we'd share a tent. The thrum of downpour matched our hungry mouths. Blau covered my body with generous sweat.

Hello

The porcelain doll, his older sister's, sits on the windowsill wearing a sailor dress and a goading expression. The doll has human-hair pigtails tied in pink bows plugged into its cranium. Peach-colored skin. A cat named Salsa suns itself next to her. The boy holds a ball-peen hammer over the doll's head. Salsa jumps to the floor and curls up in a bean bag chair.

The boy growls at the doll. *You're ugly and you're nothing and you're held together with glue.* The doll stares. The boy lays down his hammer and gnaws on his thumbnail.

His sister's nightgown lies sprawled across her bed. It's white and silky, with sleeves frilled at the wrists. He loves how the hem brushes the floor when his sister wears it. How tiny her feet look beneath it. He touches it. The house hums.

Slipping the gown over his coveralls and T-shirt, the boy closes his eyes and twirls. The cat and the doll watch. He looks at himself in the full-length mirror, stands nose-to-nose with his reflection. He touches his cheeks. He touches the mirror. *Hello,* he says.

Pets: Three Vignettes

1. I was riding LBJ's horse bareback when it
    jumped off the cliff. This was no surprise, as
    she'd pulled the same stunt once before, into the
    Rio Grande. Still I was more prepared this time,
    wore my striped bathing cap from the Five &
    Ten and had practiced plunging into our pond
    from a platform my daddy built when he wasn't
    at the local bar. I tell ya, if it wasn't for 4-H, I'd
    be on some other planet like Pluto, where they
    don't even have horses, looking for a missing
    rope to tie myself up through nine lives.

2. I can't recall whose idea it was. We were tired of
    the typical Christmas: candy canes, mistletoe,
    especially the tree. Who really enjoys cutting
    them down? Lumberjacks. And even though
    Mom used to be in forestry, I think it was Uncle
    Stan who suggested the kitty tree. At first it
    sounded like huh? Then, when he drew the pho-
    to, all black cats piled atop one another like the

Dallas Cowboy Cheerleaders in perfect formation, those eyes glaring like a taxidermist's nightmare, the blackness of the holiday seemed perfect. Little Mina started to race around the living room peeing her pants in excitement, while the rest of us shouted yes!

3. Ever since the Sonoma earthquake, we've started eating in the shower. You can accomplish two things simultaneously. Hana insists we eat out of rubberized cat dishes and since both of our kitties were flattened in the rubble, I suppose it's a way to honor them. But Hana gets claustrophobic and bossy sometimes, blurts things like, "Eat this!" When she does, I push her face into the oatmeal. Sometimes she laughs, but usually she says it's like being raped without the r. I just smirk, tell her don't be such a pussy.

Love Train ~ Lifelike ~ Spill

Love Train

Rodney and Chelsea sit close in the back seat. Chelsea's mom is listening to something from the 70s. She's singing along, bopping in the driver's seat, as Rodney travels his hand up Chelsea's thigh. Rodney hooks his index finger into her shorts. Both of them are staring straight ahead. He wiggles his finger up into her and Chelsea closes her eyes, wanders her own small hand over the bump in Rodney's shorts. The three of them had been hiking all morning and both Rodney and Chelsea are a little sweaty. Rodney leans over and kisses Chelsea's shoulder blade. It tastes salty. Chelsea's mom glances back at them and meets Rodney's eyes.

Lifelike

"I want to be an artist," Chelsea announces to her mother, who is doing squats in the basement, swinging a kettle bell. Her mother goes "FOO" every time she hoists the kettle bell forward.

Chelsea says. "I'm really excited about Expressionism. That stuff speaks to me."

"FOO."

"I'm making dioramas of Great Women from World History. Amelia Earhart. Eleanor Roosevelt. I'm using all those Easter bunnies Dad has been giving me. I expect an A."

Chelsea's mother sets down the kettle bell and tightens her ponytail. "Well! Sounds different. Oh, you know who's good at art? Your brother, Royal."

Chelsea's mother digs around in some boxes in the storage space, excavates a worn piece of construction paper with a drawing of what looks to Chelsea like a cow with a horn.

"It's a rhino. How perfect is that? See, the teacher wrote *very lifelike* on it."

Spill

Let me try to draw this for you. I'm no artist, that's why I'm a doctor. Ha ha! This is what your uterus looks like. It's a very unhappy uterus! And here—are your fallopian tubes and these—are your ovaries. For most women they're tiny but yours are huge! And this is a fibroid ON your uterus! The size of a grapefruit! And right here is your cervix! I say we take it all! You'll feel so much better! You'll be up and walking around the very next day! You're a perfect candidate! No more periods! I'm jealous of you!

The gynecologist looks so happy. Chelsea's mother is confused. She has always longed to be a perfect candidate for something. She digs around for the tin of Altoids in her purse. Her hands operate in a scattershot fashion, independent of her brain. Everything spills.

BREACH

The act or a result of breaking; break or rupture.

Tool

She no longer recognizes herself. Even her voice has changed. She moves, walks, and talks exactly like her grandmother did. She feels lumpy, angry, deranged. She has begun Facebook stalking Rodney, her daughter's boyfriend.

All the clothes are cuter in the Junior's section. She may be 42, but she's not ready for mom jeans. She still has stitches from her Total Hysterectomy. She is still a little puffy. The surgeon removed a tumor the size of a grapefruit, so why does she look six months pregnant? Her gynecologist told her it may take upwards of six months to get back to normal. A fact she failed to share before the surgery. Chelsea's mother comes out of the dressing room wearing a short dress with cap sleeves and flowers all over it. She peers into the full-length mirror. The teenager standing there looks up from her phone and rolls her eyes.

Chelsea finds her mother sitting at the kitchen table looking into a large book.

"What are you reading?"

"It's the dictionary. I'm losing nouns. I'm trying to find them."

"You're losing nouns." Chelsea pours herself a glass of chocolate milk.

"Last night I couldn't think of the word for the tool you use to open a bottle of wine."

"Corkscrew."

"Right. But I couldn't think of it. Then I was sitting in traffic on my way to work this morning and it popped into my head. Corkscrew!"

"Mom..."

Chelsea's mother reads from the dictionary: "Fissure. Fuck. Fuck's a noun. Ha. Of course it is. Fudge. Fuel. A few pages every day. I feel so fucking demented. Dementia. There's a noun for you."

"I wanted to ask you about something."

"Furze. A prickly evergreen shrub."

"Mom. Look at me. Rodney wants you to stop sending him pictures."

Chelsea's mother turns her face to the window. "Furze," she says. "I pricked myself on the furze."

Postcards of a Life

When I left home, for numerous reasons, I never looked back. My father sent me postcards.

The first one was a cockatoo perched in a cage. The slogan read, If You Can't Afford the Vet, You Can't Afford the Pet. He had scrawled, *Why are you ignoring us?* In his barely legible handwriting I mistook for, *Why are you boring us?*

By the time I received his second postcard, I was married, working endless hours at my taxidermy business. On the front was a photo of Whistler's Mother. Not an arbitrary choice, nothing my father did ever was. I knew that Whistler had only referred to this painting as "Arrangement in Grey and Black." So, I was not surprised when I flipped over the postcard to read, *Your mother left me.*

A new decade brought the third, a stunning color photograph of the sunset at Waikiki beach. The front had HAWAII embossed in silver letters. He wrote, *Mai Tai's and bikinis galore, wish you were here.*

The year I turned sixty, I got the fourth, a week before my birthday. I almost tossed it out with the junk mail. It was a completely black front, no picture, no logo. I turned it over, an invitation to his funeral.

Peacock

Her daughter, Janey, had the flu, so Tess had to take care of her and watch the film about the mermaid, but she wanted to go to the man, who waited in his apartment on the other side of town. She kept asking Janey if she was maybe feeling a little better and the girl shivered under her electric blanket, looking both dull and panicked.

Let's take your temperature again. Janey's medicine made her smell like peaches. Tess had gone to the expense of having her legs waxed and now she sat on the sofa wearing a sweater and boxers, running her hand up and down the cool smoothness, imagining her hand was the man's hand. She went into the other room to phone him, but got his message. She loved the sound of his voice. She lay on the bed and let herself think about it awhile.

When she came back, the mermaid had legs and was dancing with a prince. She'd seen this movie before

116

but couldn't remember how the mermaid got her legs. The man Tess was dating looked a little like this prince if the prince were older and bald. When the phone had beeped, the only message Tess could think to leave was *please*.

Janey's fever rose and now she was sitting up, teeth chattering. *There's a peacock in the kitchen,* she whispered.

No, no, there is no peacock in the kitchen, darling. Tess thought she might carry Janey upstairs, lower her into a tub of cool water. When Janey was nine months old, her temperature had spiked in the car outside the doctor's office. Tess heard an ungodly, animal noise and turned around to see Janey's eyes roll back, her arms and legs jerking. She didn't look like a baby anymore. She looked like something mechanical.

The kitchen curtains had a paisley pattern, bright blue. Tess pointed. *There's your peacock, sweetie.* Janey lay back down, pulled the blanket to her chin.

Tess went to Janey and held her hand. It burned. The phone began to ring. She let it.

Sometimes the man drove over to the nearby town and played pool in the bars. He liked the people there better. No pressure. He said it felt like a getaway.

Tess closed her eyes and a negative image of Janey's face swam behind her eyelids. She thought it might be good to sleep awhile. Maybe curl up under the blanket with Janey. The phone stopped and the mermaid was singing. Before she sprouted legs, and because her longing was so terrible, the mermaid collected objects from the dry and mysterious world, treasuring them and keeping them secret.

Dew Drop Inn

I was late to the square dance for guys with O.C.D. It was fully underway but before I stepped into the bar, I had to circle back to my car thirty steps one way, three times, circle the car three times, thirty steps total, then click my alarm beeper three times off/on, off/on, off/on. Ah, better.

I'd hoped they'd all be in two straight lines, the way we used to choose partners in gym class. It'd been ages since I'd square danced, or danced at all. But Benny said, *C'mon, you'll have fun. All the guys are a blast.*

He waved to me from the floor. I don't wave, it confuses people. As I hung up my coat, I did a quick scan, counting heads, relieved to find there were thirty-six dancers, four couples formed nine squares, but the caller made me anxious.

I joined Benny. The first song was Abba, and everybody sang along. I abhor pop music. Only listen to

119

waltzes and was hoping we'd start with the Blue Danube. Benny reminded me it's not Ballroom Dancing. He led me around the circle while the barker called things out of alphabetical order, like "heads promenade" (fourteen letters, shit!) before "allemande left" (same...fuck!)

Just didn't make sense. Felt like two left feet, or fifteen toes or I'm just not cut out for this inane activity in a room filled with bumbling automatons.

Grip

I pull up to the street outside my brother Mike's house and cut the engine. I sit back for a bit, still harnessed in my seatbelt, and watch the men pulling shingles off his roof and flinging them to the ground. It's late March and they're in T-shirts, but there's frost on the grass. Steam from their breath like low-lying clouds. The sun has not shone once since I arrived a week ago.

Finally I get out and approach the house, waving my arms. They halt their work long enough for me to get inside. I confront a small boy in overalls, holding a toy hammer, his cheeks tender and rosy like a picture-book child.

One of them couldn't get a sitter, Mike says, coming up behind me with a cup of dry Cheerios for the kid. Mike works from home. He has three computers in his office, a stand-up desk with a treadmill. I'm afraid he's going to ask me to stay and watch the kid, but I have things I need to do, funeral errands, like going to Walgreens to have prints made from the old pictures we'll display, and getting Easter lilies for the chapel. Our brother Tom died a couple of days ago and his daughter requested these things, gave all of her dad's siblings some tasks. He is being cremated as we speak.

The boy sits on the kitchen floor with his Cheerios and his hammer and stares at me. Drool streams from his lower lip. The noise overhead gets louder, as if the workers have ceased pulling shingles and are now letting loose with hammers and clubs and steel-toed boots. Mike and I look at the ceiling.

And why must this be done today? I ask my brother. He sips his coffee. *If I cancel it'll be weeks before they can come back.*

The boy smiles at me. I do not smile back.

I wonder how it's possible that a living breathing person can be gripping your hand one day and reduced to a pile of ashes the next. We all stood around his bed at the hospice, my other brothers and I, and Tom grabbed hold of my hand and gripped it hard enough to hurt. He was smiling, had a gleam in his eye.

Mike said, *You've still got it, bro.* Tom had been a quarterback, a state wrestling champion. My dad used to have the boys squeeze tennis balls while they watched TV. Grip was important. The difference between winning and losing.

Tom had stopped talking the day before. Was given no more fluids per the protocol. Massive amounts of morphine and anti-seizure meds were being pumped into his body, but the hand gripping mine was warm and strong.

Take it easy, you'll break her hand, my brother Steve said. We all laughed. This was one of those good moments from the last few days. There'd been others. When Tom's ex-wife leaned in close to him, smiling, and he wrapped his arms around her. When the college buddy showed up, had driven all the way from Texas and sat next to Tom telling all the old, wild stories. The fight they got into in a small town bar and the night they spent in jail there, being fed pork barbecue and corn on the cob and not wanting to leave. The stories made Tom laugh, albeit soundlessly. It was so good to see.

He finally let go and lay back. Steve dipped the tiny sponge on a stick into the bottle of Crown Royal and dabbed it on Tom's lips and tongue. *Here, brother*, he said, *have some of the good stuff.*

Dehydration

Every letter was a love letter. Except the last one.

Before you left, I had volumes, an entire box filled with "I love you" or "you're the best Dad," and "I miss you so much."

But the last letter, with the ebony embossed heading at the top: Schirmer & Sons Funeral Home, didn't even have a signature. Didn't even have a name written for whom it was addressed.

Where did you go? I knew that often a woman, all grown up, drifts down her long hair and is lost. But how did you end up in Maui, an international surfing champion? Of course, there was your love of water. Your mother had the hardest time getting you out of tubs and pools, your lips turned blue, fingers furrowed, shivering with inner chill.

Then you stopped calling...

Was it him? Did he hurt you? The papers say it was more than one man, a gang of men who did this. How is that possible? I cannot rest.

Recently your mother wanted to get rid of everything of yours, she didn't tell me at first. But I sensed it was coming. I'd already taken the first five or six letters you wrote, when you'd moved to New York, met your first roommate, auditioned for that off-Broadway play. Invited us to opening night.

Those crickety seats, watching you as Desdemona. The air stopped while you transformed. How it sounded, after a scene or two, that you'd always been her.

I hear you, even now, saying oh, dad. Dad.

I'm still here.

Pulse

Jack said his old Grenada was mine if I could jump-start it. He wished me luck as he handed over the cables. We dated for three years. Broke up last week, after a party. The police had found him naked and throwing insults and tennis balls at people from the roof of the old Black's department store. My friend Pansy drove me over to his house so I could use her battery for the jump.

A bowl of bread dough sat rising in a sunny corner. The whole place smelled of yeast. Jack was slicing mushrooms thin as petals with a paring knife. He was always at his most attractive when he was cooking. His pit bull, Magnum, shuffled around, bumping into things. He plopped down in the middle of the kitchen floor.

Pansy said, "You should have this animal put down." She knelt and laid her hand on his abdomen. "His bowels are distended."

Jack wiped his hand on a dishtowel. "So the car probably needs new tires. The horn doesn't work. Passenger side door can only be opened from the outside."

I'd spent my last dime bailing him out of jail. I'd ridden in it a few times. I knew it was a piece of crap, but the car was payback.

Pansy stood, eyeing him. "You don't like me much do you?"

"You stole my girlfriend."

Jack's Grenada was stretched out on the overgrown grass of his front yard like a larger version of Magnum. Pansy eased her Rav-4 over the curb and parked alongside it. I let her hook up the cables and I slid in behind the wheel. She started her car. I waited a bit, then turned the key. Click, click, click. I looked over at her, shrugged.

"Try again," she called over to me.

I turned the key again. The engine roared.

We had to step over Magnum, who was now lying on the front porch, his eyes closed. Jack signed over the registration and handed it to me.

Pansy folded her arms. "You should check his pulse."

Something was simmering on the stove. A sauce, with mushrooms, onions, and butter. I wanted a taste.

The Literary Savant

After I bring her back to the house, I show her my new temporary license. I look like a demented tard. Or a fat ex-con who gained a hundred pounds in prison eating chips and bean dip while watching Judge Judy re-runs.

"I would date a dog," she says.

"Really?" I squeeze the fresh limes into our drinks. "Any particular breed?"

She shrugs. "German Shepherds and herding dogs. Not those little ones that sometimes jump out of wedding cakes."

But when I show her photos of a Border Collie her nose wrinkles. She says, "Did you know that it's illegal to harass a seeing-eye dog?"

It reminds me of my recent fruit fly infestation. I tell her how I forgot I'd left the balsamic vinegar on the counter the entire July 4th weekend I was in the Wisconsin Dells. Mom told me to put the bowl in the microwave and leave the door open. After the fruit flies all rush in there, slam the door, fifteen seconds. Zap!

She sips her gin and tonic. "Bet it smelled like pork chops."

"More like a reduction sauce."

We're sitting on my back patio, and it's getting cozy with my baby until a mechanical repetitive sound, disturbing and oddly melodic, starts up. "They're fracking at my neighbor's house," I joke. "Maybe we can sneak into their pool when it's finished?"

"That's not funny," she says. "If I didn't have a passive yeast resistance condition I could be the next Heidi Fleiss of the Midwest."

"My cousin Helga moved to Switzerland last year for a sex change—and she, well, *he* said just avoid that cheese with the holes."

While she chews her ice, I think of the Three Stooges, trying to decide if I look more like Curly or Larry. Then it dawns on me, who I look like in my damn license. "Hey—ever hear of Tolstoy?"

She fingers the ice around in her glass. "Is that some other kind of cheese I have to avoid?"

The Four O'Clock Bird

The child knows the man with the patch over his eye is not really going to buy him a hamburger. He feels the man's heavy hands on his shoulders. The child is wearing his best red coat and cap, but he is shivering. The man coughs and says, *Smile*. The child refuses. The child starts to say something to the photographer, but the photographer seems to be a friend of the man's.

His mother would say they were in cahoots. It's cold. Near dusk. And they are in a sooty alleyway and now the man wants him to smile for the camera. The man had said hello to him when he was out in the garden playing. The man showed him a toy owl. The child loves birds. How did the man know? His mother had said she would be back from the store in five minutes. She told him to hum every song he knew and she'd be back before he finished. She would bring him something sweet.

So the boy hummed and played in the garden and came closer when the man asked him to. He so wanted to hold the toy owl. To pet its feathers. The man said he could if he was a good boy and held his hand. Now the man was grasping his shoulders and the child was shivering and the photographer said, *It's okay, I don't need him to smile,* and both of the men laughed. Not far away, the child heard the bird who was not an owl. The solitary bird who sang every afternoon at the same time no matter what. Its song reminded him not to cry. To be brave. He would swivel his head around just like an owl and he would bite the man's rough hand very hard.

Keep It Curt

Every time I told Curt to keep it.
Keep it closed, I'd say. Cut it out!
Or keep it to yourself, Curt.
He didn't like me telling him.
He was not in favor of seasonal dictation.
And Curt would say, I have my heart.
And I'd say, keep it, Curt!
This was way before Tammy. And before Trinidad &
Tobago.
And before he fucked my mother. And Gladys
Knight.
Before he was really someone, you know?
I'm not sorry, he'd say. (Sorry for what?)
Keep it, Curt, I'd say. Sometimes, not always.
When we broke up, he'd say, hey—that doily is mine.
Or that painting of the Native Americans.
Fine. Keep it, Curt.
Just move the fuck out.
When he tried to claim our extensive dildo collection,
I put my foot down.

I'll take you to court, Curt said.
Fine, keep it, Curt.
I know I'd have to pay all the fees.
That was Curt. Cheap as fuck.

Sea Creatures of Indiana

Benny's teaching me to French inhale under the street light outside Dairy Queen. It's his last night before he goes up North to some little college his dad went to.

I'd been craving a dip cone and now we're passing the dip cone and a joint back and forth, taking turns on each. The dip cone's drooping.

"Blow it out your mouth," Benny says. "Now. Suck the smoke in deep. No, through your nose, brainless."

I'm doing it all wrong but getting high as shit regardless. The dip cone looks like Mick Jagger.

Benny knows what he wants to do with his life. I envy that. It's something to do with marine biology, but more specific than that.

"Benny, my friend, I just realized something very key." I start to laugh, then cough. Laugh. Cough.

He pitches the dip cone and pulls me out of the light, to a picnic table recently vacated by a couple and their two kids. Plunks me down. I set my elbow in a puddle of melted ice cream. We sit gazing at each other in the dark. He's French inhaling like a pro.

"What did you realize, burnout?" he asks.

My train of thought has left the station. Benny has a boyfriend, Jon, his dad doesn't know about. Or maybe he does. But I'm Benny's best friend. His only girl friend.

The manager comes out with a broom, starts to sweep up wrappers, cigarette butts, a few fallen leaves. He comes over.

"You two better beat it," he says. Benny and I crack up. I am practically falling off the picnic table. The manager standing there in his paper hat, aiming that broom at us like a rifle. Jesus Christ.

"Take your marijuana and go," he says, but he calls it mari-JEW-ana. We are dying.

Then walking real fast. I stop and lean on a tree.

"I've got it," I say.

"What?"

"Benny do you realize there's no ocean in Indiana?"

He's looking at me. He's super tall and I'm super short. One Halloween we went as Ketchup and Mustard. Mustard's always the small one.

"Right?" I say. "I mean, why do they even have a marine biology program there?"

Benny says, *fuck*. Real slow.

I want to keep talking. To talk so fast he'll have no choice but to listen to me. I want to remind him about Jon. What happens when people move far away? They drift. They float apart. And Benny's dad. He knows, right? How could he not?

Now we're at our old elementary school and it's getting chilly, but we're swinging on the swings anyway. Benny's standing on his. These guys drive by and yell out their window.

"Faggots!"

We know these guys. We graduated with them. They call me a faggot too. I'm a girl with super short hair who dresses like a guy. I get it.

They're slowing down.

I yell back, "Hey do you guys want to French inhale?"

I guess they take it wrong.

Now they're flying out of that car. Benny leaps off the swing, his long legs pumping, but they're upon him. One of them pulls me off my swing and has me on the ground, on the new, spongy surface all the playgrounds have now.

Nobody gets hurt on playgrounds anymore.

I'm being punched repeatedly. There's a rhythm to it. *Flump, flump, flump.* I feel nothing. I only hear Benny screaming and it sounds too far away. Just before I lose consciousness I realize he's not calling Mom, Mom, Mom but...*Jon, Jon, Jon.*

Now Benny's studying sea creatures in a computer lab at that college. Jon and I never hear from him. Indiana has swallowed him whole. Jon works at the Sunglass Hut at the mall and he says he will never love anyone else. Ever.

Yesterday I took myself on a field trip to the aquarium downtown. I even packed a lunch, like a fourth grader. My favorite are the sea urchins. The hedgehogs of the sea. But to me, sea urchins are the spiny punk rockers of the sea. They latch on to tiny rocks and shells or seaweed or coral. They decorate themselves with all manner of stuff, and for a while, they look like something else entirely. Benny said that's how they keep themselves safe.

Four Stone Cups

The cab driver did not slow down for a deep pothole. My iPhone sailed out the open window, into the adjacent lane of traffic cramming like sardines down 7th Avenue South.

"Fuck! Hey!" I shouted, rapping the plexiglass separating the front and back seats.

He looked in his rear view, his turban loomed, transporting me to my uncle Dex's cabin in Sonoma. Dex reading *Ali Baba and the 40 Thieves*. My uncle's hand on my thigh. My uncle who died before he turned 30.

"Pull over," I shouted. "Stop the cab!"

Abdul slowed and we stopped. I looked out and saw the Joyce Theater- we were in Chelsea. It was 3 a.m., and without my phone I was lost. Stuck. What was his address? I pulled the slip of paper out of my pocket with his name and telephone number on it. Who was he anyhow?

The cab driver waited, double parked. I fished for a ten in my shorts, the small pocket change landing all over the back seat and filthy floor of the cab. I handed the bill to him through the glass. "Keep the change," I said. As I got out, I looked back to see Abdul grinning.

It only took me twenty minutes to cut over to the East Village on 14th Street. I was starving, and followed my nose right to Ray's Pizza on St. Mark's, ordered a slice and stood at the greasy window staring at the people streaming by like a zombie.

"Busy night?" A guy in a white sailor uniform stood in the cavity beside me. He was eating a mushroom slice and grinning. His jet black closely-cropped curls were a startling contrast to his entirely white get-up. Oddly, I felt under-dressed.

I nodded. "Lost my phone."

"That sucks," he said, handing me a napkin. "I'm Tony."

"Michael," I lied. He held out his hand, and I shook it, despite how greasy mine felt. His grip was firm, and I then noticed how strong he was. "Are you on leave?"

He nodded, as he glommed down his last bite. "Let's get out of here?"

I knew the apartment was on E. 6th Street and once I saw the Indian restaurants all lined up in a row, I had my bearings. Dad had told me to just scan the rooftops- it's the building with the four cups. I thought Tony was just killing time keeping me company, but when we got to my door, he stood there. "May I use your bathroom?"

"Sure." My keys worked in both doors, and we took the stairs to the fifth floor, no elevator. My heart was pumping, and I opened the apartment door. All of my things were in boxes around the studio, and I smiled. "The bathroom's off the kitchen," I pointed out for Tony. There was a note on the table.

Buddy Boy- here is the place that your Uncle Dex left you in his will. Be kind to the space, it's been in our family for decades. So many of us have lived here, including

Dex, he'd be so happy that you'll now call it home. Your mother and I hope your first semester at NYU goes swell. Knock them dead! We love you, Dad

I heard Tony washing up, and stuffed the note in my pocket. He came out of the bathroom, and we stood there, staring at one another. "Let's go up on the roof?"

We stood in the dense night air, the city humming below. The Empire State Building still displayed 4th of July colors. Patriotic. A sailor. Despite it being warm, I shivered.

"Cold?" Tony asked.

I shrugged. "My name's not Michael," I confessed. "It's Guy."

He smiled. "That's okay. I'm not on leave either. I deserted."

I wasn't entirely sure what that meant. "We'd better find you some civilian clothes," I said.

"You and I might be close to the same size?"

He was being kind. I stared at the Cups, the stone chalices that marked the four corners of the building. Tony came up behind me, took me in his arms, pulling me against him. "Guy," he whispered, his lips just brushing my earlobe.

River

We could have stayed at the lodge, but my husband
said what we needed was wide open space. Then, delay upon delay, we arrived after dark, grateful for the
full moon and the campfires dotting the grounds to
light the way to our spot.

We'll pitch a tent tomorrow, he said. *Tonight, we'll sleep
under the stars. That big moon.*

The girls stood with their eyes closed and arms out as
I encased them in a cloud of bug spray. They wanted
their sparklers. *Dinner first,* I said. We built a fire, set a
lantern ablaze. Heated beans on the cookstove. Skew-
ered hot dogs.

After we ate, I climbed a hillside to meditate. Meditation, my doctor told me, was the best cure for what
ailed me. *You're not clinically depressed,* he said. I'd
been hoping for drugs.

The cool felt good. The limbs of the cottonwood trees swayed and intertwined. I found a spot and sat for a long time, listening to the sounds of the campers laughing and talking. Eventually their voices grew quiet, sleepy.

I was thinking too much, forgetting to breathe slowly.

One trick of meditation is to imagine yourself seated at the bank of a river. The river is your thoughts. You observe them and let them flow on by. I thought of my husband's tone earlier in the car, his too-annoyed response when I'd only asked if he remembered the jackets. Impatience out of scale, like bad acting. The girls stayed quiet around him these days.

I heard footsteps and turned. An old guy in just shorts. His white legs glowing. A cap on his head.

You startled me, I said.

Sorry, young lady.

No, it's cool. I should get back.

He took my hand and helped me up. We headed back down the hill.

He said he was here with his wife and grandkids. They came every year. I told him I had two daughters. *And a husband*, I said.

He stopped and cupped his hands around his mouth.

Ow ow ow ow ow ow owwwwww, he called. And far off, I heard a smaller voice, *owwwwwww owwww.*

My grandson, he said. *We pretend we're wolves.*

It seemed a lovely thing to me, to call out into the darkness and have someone call back to you like that. Like, hi, I'm here. And ok, I'm a wolf.

I could tell the old man's knees were hurting him so I slowed down.

Up there, where I was sitting? I said. *I was trying to imagine a river.*

Rivers are nice.

We were getting closer. At first I could only see the sparklers. The spitting, electric fire looping and dancing, making letters in the air. The girls were invisible, but their names emerged and hung suspended, bright and shining, long enough for me to read them.

Picnic

My aunts and uncles and cousins by the dozens are at the 4th of July picnic. I wasn't going to come, Vermont's too far now that I live in Seattle. And two tickets were too pricey. But this might be Dad's last year. And there's no better time to introduce Trisha, my new spouse, twenty years my junior.

Everyone is so fucking polite. I'm reduced to Ricky, not Richard. Aunt Flo has gained fifty pounds. Uncle Dirk's skin is blue from his pacemaker. We're all hanging in the backyard tent which makes the 100 degree heat feel like 110. I have to pee so I head inside the house. On the back porch, I hear Mom blabbing with Aunt Jo in the kitchen, so I pause.

"She seems awfully nice," Mom says. "Trisha."

"My gawd, Deanna," Aunt Jo says, "He could be her father."

I don't know whether to interrupt them, or head back outdoors and pee on Aunt Jo's prize-winning rose bushes.

Go Dog

The woman's lover died quickly and unexpectedly on his front porch. He'd been drinking whiskey and now the sun was low and shown on his dead face. His dog licked his chest, right above the spot where his heart had seized up, until his wife came and found him. She put her hand to her mouth, collected the bottle and the broken bits of glass, and went inside to make the calls she had to make.

In his will, her lover had stipulated that should he die before his dog, he wanted the dog to go to her. It didn't make sense. She didn't like dogs. She didn't like *Shep*. When her lover came to her place, it was always under the pretense of walking Shep, so Shep of course had to come along. The dog scratched at the bedroom door while they had sex.

When she came to pick up the dog, her lover's wife said, "I'm so sad, but I don't like this dog. I'm glad he'll have a good home." As far as the wife knew, she had just been her husband's friend and coworker at Food Land.

She opened the car door for the dog, who loped in with his tail down. The dog looked like a wolf and she didn't like wolves. She sat in the car in front of her lover's house and watched his widow move from room to room, up the stairs and down. She watched for a long time and then she drove away.

Immediately she changed the dog's name to Bill. That was her lover's name. But, the dog never came to "Bill." The dog stared when she said "Bill." He cocked his head to one side, like *what?*

At night, she tried on looks—bored looks or smart looks or amused looks—before the bathroom mirror. She put on the hat she wore to the funeral, pulled the netting over her face.

"Do you like my hat?" she said to the dog. "Bill? Bill!" The dog lifted his eyes, but kept his chin planted on the floor. She threw the hat in the sink and ran water over it, as if it were on fire.

When she retired for the evening, the dog stood by the bed and whined.

"So he slept with you, too, eh?" She dragged the dog by the collar to the hallway. "Sleep here," she said. And she went back to bed and hummed. Every night, she burrowed under the covers and hummed and rocked from side to side. The dog scratched at the door. "Go, dog," she murmured, vibrating with grief until dawn.

Her friends from Food Land, who worked with Bill too, liked to talk about him after work at The 929. How he had been so kind and smart and how he helped so much. How he didn't mind doing a price check once in a while, or replacing a carton of eggs. All this, even though he was the manager. But she knew this to be a little untrue. Bill could be a prick. But she'd listen on, remembering the feel of him between her legs, his whiskers against her cheek, and she'd remark coolly that he certainly *was* a nice guy and a good boss and they'd sip their beers and nod.

As the months passed, she noticed her house filling up with the smell of dog, a smell she associated with Bill, his visits, their sex. She lit candles, sprayed deodorizer, opened windows. Finally, she gave the dog a bath in her tub. Her hands shook as she squeezed the handle of the sprayer and she missed the dog, showering the walls.

"Bill! Bill!" she shouted. The dog barked and she dropped the sprayer on the floor. She sat on the side of the tub until the dog started to shiver and whine. "Shit," she said, and hoisted him out and toweled him off. Later, when she was brushing her teeth she noticed how the veins in the backs of her hands had grown bulgy as worms, as if she had been turned inside out.

Once she and Bill had taken a ferry ride together. It was an impulsive, risky act, but they held hands in line and a photographer made everybody stop before they boarded and have their picture taken. At the end of the trip, the photos were displayed in a kiosk for purchase. She'd wanted to stop and take a look at least, but Bill pulled her along past the crowd. She wanted that photo now, to put it in a nice frame and set it next to her bed. She wanted it for the same reason Bill didn't: Photos make things real.

It snowed all night and was still snowing next morning, but she bundled herself and took the dog out. He kept his tail low, sniffed and pawed, moved slow.

"We lack zest, Bill," she told him. She thought she might get him one of those jaunty sweaters some people put on their dogs.

She had seen her lover rub the dog's chin and neck. She tried it. He lifted his nose and closed his eyes. She patted the top of his head, his ears. She knelt in the snow and held his face in her hands. The flakes on his brow gave him a wizened look. She took off her gloves and buried her fingers in his fur. It felt as though they were both sinking into a crevasse. The man across the street, who had been shoveling, called over to her. *Can I help you? Is everything all right?*

It was the kind of wet snow that wanted melting right away, the kind that preceded the sudden, glad appearance of spring. You only had to wait a little longer. She pressed her ear to the dog's warm side and listened.

Cosmos at Aspen

"I don't know if I can do this," I said. "How I can do this?"

"You need some stamina," Miles replied.

"Stamina? Are you serious?" I laughed. "Look at me. I can barely move." I felt like a vegetable, like the take-out noodle dish I eat nearly every night in Silver Lake.

He chuckled, slid further down into the plush sofa we shared. Stared into the car-sized fireplace. The swirling colors transfixed us.

The waitress at Embers approached us, cleavage first. "Another round?" she asked, as if she'd said, "Blow and go?"

Miles looked at me, shrugged. "I will if you will."

The cosmos were twenty bucks a pop. Welcome to Aspen. I felt my wallet become ethereal, so light I could barely feel it. "What the hell," I said, handing Cherise my empty martini glass. Imagined she'd touched my hand, held it for a second longer than she did. "Guess we're done skiing for the day?" I glanced out at skiers whizzing by the lodge, various colors blending against the white backdrop. The snow screamed, it was so bright.

We sat in silence, the fire crackling, a constant steam noise, more like a river. It reminded me of Patricia, of a kayak trip we took the first year we'd met. Near Vancouver on the Squamish River. The water was unusually high, the paddle disorganized. My kayak capsized within five minutes on our float, no guide in sight. Patricia bailed from hers, rescuing me from potential disaster. Now I felt like I was in that same jam, drowning. Just in some other way. Don't think about her, I told myself.

Not now.

"Hey, where'd ya go?" Miles asked, slapping my knee. He must have seen the look on my face. "Aw, don't go there, man. Not now."

I leaned my head back against the couch. "What am I supposed to do? Pretend she's still here?"

The Possibility of Bears

We'd been drinking wine and eating leftover wedding cake on the deck. I'd chosen rainbow colored frosting. It was supposed to taste like strawberries.

"I shouldn't be drinking," I said.

"Then stop."

We were staying in a cabin in a national forest. The first thing we saw as we lugged our suitcases from the car were claw marks on the door. I asked if they were real. He said he suspected so.

Behind the cabin was a cornfield, which seemed out of place. I had wanted to go to Switzerland, but this place was okay. Cheaper.

He started cleaning up.

I said, "Well, look at that view."

He wetted his finger and opened a garbage bag.

"Gosh, you're so fastidious," I said, but it came out wrong, sounded more like facetious. I read the label on the wine. A peppery finish, it said.

He reminded me about the possibility of bears.

I watched him sweep, moving in and out of the shadows. I tried to think if we'd been to any movies lately. There was an old style movie house five miles down the road in the little town, showing The Three Stooges.

"We could try to find Stephen King's vacation house," I said.

He continued to sweep.

"I think you can stop now," I said.

I pointed out the hot tub, but his head was turned to some noise in the woods. He said, "I'm not exactly a Boy Scout."

"Neither am I."

Like wine, the hot tub was probably not good for me either.

He sat down. I toed off my slippers, forked cake into his mouth.

"Eat this," I said. "Eat every last bite." And he chewed and stared. When we were first living together, we used to do this. Feed each other. Lick things off each other's bodies. After the ceremony he'd found some emails. I said they were old. But they weren't old enough. And now here we were. Married.

"Wait. I hear it now."

"That's the sound of a bear protecting its baby."

I heard it again. Closer.

"Cub," I said.

No Face World Champ

He had a thing for gimps. Scanning pages of Paralympic competitors, surfers riding the shark munch waves. He'd cut out photos of stumps, prosthetics, limbs that were missing, unattached, removing more and more in his mind until he was rubbing a rubbed out image. Shadows of his former wheelchaired marathon racers, downhill ski racers with singular poles. The last time he saw his psychic, she told him you're gonna die within six months. Her prediction nearly took over his fantasies of stubby limbs, of one-eyed jacks, of spinal biffs. Instead, he started a support group for People With Missing Limbs (PWML) and posted it all over the social networks, and craigslist. The first meeting attracted a large crowd, but he was completely unprepared to respond when Patty, a dwarf who had gone through recent gender reassignment, whose toddler feet had done a tango with a lawnmower, asked him, "So what are you doing here?"

CATACLYSM

*A sudden and violent physical action producing changes
in the earth's surface.*

Me and You and a Voice Named Boo

In the attic, behind the crawl space there was a hole. And when you lay in bed that October, you could hear whispers, people calling your name. Darrin. Sometimes it sounded like Davin. Or Desmond.

A dark little purr.
From the blackness.
And, silence.

Then just before Thanksgiving, you were let go from Circuit City. They called it downsizing, and you re-framed it: perks! In your last two weeks you absconded with fourteen iPods, six iMacs, a few flat screen TVs, some watches, and a gamebox (that'll last you a year).

Your last night home from work: at 3 a.m.!

Calling your name: Darrin. You went to the hole. It had grown, so you slid through it. Inside there were

165

mirrored walls and screens projecting different parts of your life: the cupola in Corn Hill. The snowflakes swirling around you and Joe, like in a globe. A written confession: Do blind men have visual dreams? And the large screen showing that recurring scene in which J tells you his suicide came five, almost six years later. But you'd moved on long before then. Long before it all came tumbling down. Before you dressed in dressing, versed in verses, popular with Pop-Tarts.

You'd like to think it isn't a black and white thing, but it is.

Everything's Shitty at Price King

Six minutes to closing, almost midnight. I'm alone facing shelves at Price King. The place is shitty and dirty and small. We get like three customers a day. People looking for Pampers or a gallon of milk who haven't heard of a Seven-Eleven. Buffalo Bill, the owner, inherited this place from his dad. Bill hasn't bothered to show up yet and I'm just about to finish and clock out when a man walks in holding a gun—and a baby.

He doesn't look much older than me, maybe in his early twenties, kind of bedraggled and wild-eyed in thick glasses, but it's the baby that's making it hard for me to breathe. The overhead lights dim, brighten, and stutter, like one of those old film reels. The man won't make eye contact with me, but the baby's staring and all of this feels weirdly like something I'll get quizzed on later.

My hand goes to the pocket of my apron, but I already know my phone's dead. My dad, who's probably asleep right now on the recliner in the family room, would be so disappointed in me—his now only child —for the sin of carrying an uncharged phone.

The man says, "Please. I need your help."

Super polite were it not for the firearm.

"I'd be happy to help, sir, if you'll just holster that gun —here, let me hold your baby for you."

"I need it out," he says. "I don't feel safe."

I hear you, dude.

The baby has two teeth on top and two on bottom and he's drooling. Teething. I step closer, reaching my arms out.

The man swings his hip, the one the baby's straddling, away from me. The baby throws his arms out and giggles. I get a mental picture of the baby without a head.

"This isn't my baby," he says.

Oh no.

"My dad'll be here any minute," I lie. My dad's not coming. He and my mother and I have been rolling off in all directions like billiard balls the last two years.

"Look," he says, "I need some stuff. I need you to push a cart and I'll fill it up. I have a long trip ahead."

Think.

The baby's trying to grab hold of the gun and the man dangles it in front of his face and pulls it away, a game of keep-away. The baby looks so much like my little brother, Cal.

"Much easier if I hold the baby while you shop."

The man stares.

"I'm good with babies." *Another lie.*

I'm looking hard into the man's eyes. They're dark and huge and wet. *Give me the baby. Give him to me.* His arm holding the gun grows slack. He lowers it to his side. Again, I reach for the baby.

"Nope," he raises the gun and points it at my face.

My arms and legs have gone numb. I'm watching the barrel of the gun flick and dance in the man's trembling hand. Where the hell is Big Bill? If this were a decent store, there'd be security cameras, some way to alert the cops, a non-inebriated manager on the premises. My parents have no idea how much time I spend alone here.

The baby reaches, hooks his fist around the bow of the man's glasses, sends them clattering. Growling, the man crouches, sets the gun and the baby on the floor to retrieve them.

High five, baby.

Cal drowned because of me, because I left him in the tub for *one second*. I see his motionless body, Mom pulling him out of the water, trying to breathe life into him on the bathroom floor.

Everything in me says, *now*. I rush in, swing my leg, and kick the gun away as hard as I can. I reach into my apron pocket and throw my cell phone the other direction. The man scrambles around, blind and confused. I scoop up the baby, feel the warm heft of him against my body and I'm running, running. Behind me, the gun goes off and to my left, a head of cauliflower explodes. He shoots again and the crappy music system that hasn't worked in months kicks on, blasting some country/western song, the kind of shit my dad listened to back when he was happy.

According to the police report, the man shot himself in the head, right there in aisle ten of Price King, the bullet passing through his brain and into one of the flickering overhead lights, as I ran with the baby pressed hard to my chest, as the baby screamed over some Merle Haggard sounding shit blasting from the speakers, as Big Bill came running in, a little drunk, freaking from the gunshot, confused as hell to see me holding a baby.

I remember sitting on the curb outside the store in the cold night air and the flashing lights for a few stunned moments making me think I was on the midway at the State Fair. Someone had thrown a blanket over me and the baby, who was sleeping now, and someone, an EMT I guess, was leaning in close, speaking to me slowly, gently tugging on the baby. *We just need to check on him, he'll be all right, you done good.* Over and over, *you done good*, until I finally let go. And my dad and mom showed up in their pajamas, wrapping themselves around me and we stood huddled in the parking lot, breathing and holding each other. I remember looking at my dad's bare feet, studying his hairy toes. And I remember how my mom, in her thick robe, felt impossibly small. Like a bird I could hold and keep safe in my hand.

Adrift

You walk around in circles then say you choose your own ground. I try my best to ride the tide unless it's too high. There is a prevailing feeling of restlessness here, a seam dividing as if anyone might come undone.

And this stilted house is a farce, waiting for the ocean to claim us both, plummeted onto glaciers that no longer exist. Sea creatures, barnacles, cannot wait to make their home inside our former abode.

The peg-legged abode transforms into make-shift raft, carries us to Irkutsk where we enroll in the State University's psychology department to study with the great *Potanin*. At night, trying to warm our bones by the lone fire pit, we translate Rasputin into our native *Tahltan*.

You still walk in circles, but without our house on stilts, there is no ground to choose. I am tethered to the planet by a fraying rope. By a slate blue porcelain sheet.

A Rift, A Stampede

Every year, the family sits together on the garage floor spread with newspapers and carves their jack-o'-lanterns. Louise, the five-year old, likes to name her pumpkins and this year has chosen the name "Mad Toaster." Her brother Bobby always names his pumpkin "Jack." Although their parents spend a great deal of time carving their own pumpkins, they don't follow this custom. For that reason, Louise doesn't cry when her parents' pumpkins shrivel up and are tossed into the compost heap. They are nameless and therefore needn't be mourned.

They can see their breath as they cut and dig and scrape. They are up to their elbows in pumpkin guts. Bobby puts the seeds in his mouth and sees how far he can spit them. He's aiming for Mad Toaster, but keeps missing. Sometimes the seeds land on his father's shirt. Bobby's father's glasses keep slipping down his nose. He uses his forearm to push them back up.

The oldest child, Roger, is in the backyard attempting to load his air rifle with gunpowder he ordered over the internet. Lately he's been trying his hand at homemade explosives. He wears his swim trunks year-round. Roger's resourceful, though not very bright.

Marta, the mother, looks up from her carving and asks, "Where's Roger?" but they are too busy to answer her. "Chandler," she says to her husband, "your glasses are smudged."

"I know, I know!" His hands are frozen. He wants to finish and go inside and sit in his armchair by the fire. He wants to read his leather-bound Shakespeare and drink a little cherry brandy from his favorite snifter. He feels uneasy and cold. Later, in bed, he will turn to Marta and she will laugh at him. The rift between them grows. They have not had sex in three years. Marta spends a lot of time in the laundry room.

She works as a bereavement counselor. Whenever Bobby tells his friends that his mom "sells coffins," she reminds him gently, "No, Bobby, they are caskets. Cas-kets." And Chandler says, "Can we change the subject?" He's sensitive about Marta's job, but consoles himself that at least she's not a mortician.

Marta convinced the owner of the funeral home to lend her a casket this year, the economy model, for the front yard. Chandler is going to dress up as a vampire. He plans to lie inside it and sit up and scream at approaching trick-or-treaters. Every day at lunchtime, he goes down to the basement of the building where he works and practices. The building sits on the site of The Great Buffalo Stampede of 1807.

He lies on the cold, greasy, floor with his eyes closed and his arms folded over his chest. It is more difficult to sit straight up with one's arms folded than he had imagined. He hollers and the noise hits the concrete walls and multiplies, thunders in his ears. The effect is satisfying.

Too Much Oxygen

I played tuba by default. None of the other brass players would switch. Something about the aperture. The
tuba was huge, a lot to carry on/off a bus, and forget
about placing it overhead. We didn't have overheads
anyhow, this was the 70s. The Waltons. Gas lines.
Leisure Suits. This was the summer I was raped.

Tuba was familiar, had the same exact fingering as the
trumpet valves, which I'd started in grade school.
Mom wouldn't let me practice in the house, said it
rattled our screen windows. I'd sit on our back patio
blowing bass notes toward our cow pasture.

They'd stare at me, chewing their cud. Probably wondering when I'd stop making that awful racket. I like
cows. They're peaceful.

Strangers stopping at our fruit and vegetable stand got an earful while they looked for a ripe cucumber. That year the word "stranger" upped a notch. Maybe two.

In 8th grade, I switched to baritone horn. Again, the fingering was familiar, and blowing that tuba had been making me pass out. Too much oxygen. Our band leader, Mr. Marks said, "We'll have to do something about that!"

When he placed his hand on my shoulder, I flinched.

Come Loose and Fly Away

It begins like this: The baby is red and wrinkled and squalling or bleating like a lamb. The baby has lots of hair or none at all. It has the face of a bulldog. Or Winston Churchill. The baby looks wise beyond his years. The baby's fists are clenched, his toes, splayed. He's terrified and vulnerable and angry.

The baby is weighed, his dimensions and poundage announced as if he were a prize bass. He is wrapped and held and cried over.

The baby grows. The baby gets fat. When the world pushes, the baby starts to push back. He smiles. He gurgles. He grabs hold of hair and glasses and noses and boobs. He is the center of the everything. He is at once all-powerful and powerless.

Divergences occur: He is advanced or he struggles or he does everything on schedule. He is the most beautiful human in any room he inhabits. He is his own person. He goes to school and makes friends. Or he makes enemies. He has happy days and sad days. Today he feels teased and injured and lonely. Another day he wins a prize.

He talks nonstop or he prefers to stay quiet. Maybe he writes or maybe he listens to music or he plays soccer or he reads books and loses himself in them for hours. Maybe he's hyper. Or lazy. He feels comfortable in his skin or he feels miserable in it.

And then.

It is a priest or a camp counselor or a piano teacher or a scout leader. It is a step-father or an uncle. It's what happens in the dark or behind closed doors or in a locker room. Maybe it feels good and he is ashamed. Or it hurts and he is both ashamed and afraid. He tells no one. It happens and it keeps happening and he doesn't know what to do.

The best parts of him begin to come loose and fly away. This is what happens when the earth spins too fast. Eventually even the core disintegrates.

Until something else takes its place. A new sort of aggressiveness his parents applaud.

He grows up to be an Achiever and a Narcissist. This looks like Leadership to the outside world. This is what it's like to be a star, to be admired and sought after. He learns to hurt first before getting hurt and this drives all of his future relationships. He is both charming and callous, wholly focused on himself and in this way he manages to forget. He rapes the girl in college who thought they were in love. He leaves behind a string of confused, broken-hearted women. He only wants the ones who don't want him and finally obtains such a woman and marries her.

He manages to recreate himself in the form of a son. His son becomes his own fresh start. He worships this son. There is nothing he won't do for him. One day, for his son, he promises to stop drinking. But meetings and therapy are for pussies. He will do it on his own.

His wife, who came to love him, learns what it means to live with a dry drunk.

After the divorce, something inside him comes unhinged. He swaddles himself in layers of clothes, paces the house until he can no longer stay awake. In his dreams, he is pursued and preyed upon. He feels large hands on his body. He feels what is shoved into his mouth. He is so very small, again.

One night he finds himself huddled and wide-eyed in the garden shed with a pistol in his hand. He has barricaded himself with the lawnmower, the weedwhacker, and a wheelbarrow. He is a gaping wound. He is what he was at the moment of his birth: Terrified and vulnerable and angry.

The metal door is pulled open and he thinks it is his own tall self standing there with the moon on his shoulders, his own eyes looking back at him. He thinks maybe he has already pulled the trigger. But no. The hands, the face, the way he ducks his head, the same, small voice, a child, a boy, an almost man. His son.

The Tangerine Ibis

I never thought it would come to this. Someone would have to pay, but the person most likely responsible was face down in a puddle, and at a quick glance, I wasn't certain was breathing. I bent over, pushed my bangs under my hat, and that's when I realized this was no puddle. No, it was more a lake, the liquid oozed from every pore. The sun bore down causing my already burnt skin to pulsate.

That's when I saw the ibis. It was standing in the water, perfectly still, scarlet. Just like a lawn ornament. I swear, it winked at me.

I debated whether to leave.

I wrenched his body from the murky water, dragged him up a knoll, and dumped his body down. I placed my lips to his, administered mouth-to-mouth until I got dizzy. Then slapped him awake. Fell back, exhausted. He lay there, twitching, eyes attempting to focus. Blood leaked from a stomach wound, drenched his shirt and soaked through to the dirt.

The ibis took flight, its huge wings beat the air, slow-motion. I stared as it became smaller, flying down the sparkling coastline. Tinier. A speck.

He groaned.

"Noel," I said, lighting a cigar. "You're back." The smoke kept the swarm of gnats off me.

"I'm soaked." He half-sat, coughed. Spat. Repeat. He looked around. "How did you-?"

"Mouth-to-mouth." I wouldn't look at him. Couldn't. Searched for the ibis.

He wiped his parched lips, half smiled. "Denny, I didn't—not on purpose. She-"

I flicked an ant off my leg, waiting, but he didn't continue. It would be the last time either of us mentioned her. I nodded. "You're full of shit, Noel. And you're lucky. See if you can stand up. I'll help you get to the jeep."

Strings

The aunt and uncle's farm, early spring, the earth smell of unsown fields, and Sunday lunch. My uncle sprawled in the recliner, his work boots raised like an affront. Burning Camel stuck to his lower lip. Snoring. The aunts and my mother drinking coffee. My aunt whispers about strange things coming out of her when she goes to the bathroom. And Mother spies us on the floor pretending to play Crazy Eights. She indicates with her cigarette the back door. All our lives we've been following that little point of fire.

We're given kites to assemble. Rickety-ass kites. Balsa wood and paper. Balls and balls of string. We tromp down the path between the trees. The field opens up to us like something born. My older brother, Bill, and his girlfriend all horny and shy with each other. They drop their kites and head for the barn.

We tear bits of colored paper, straddle them on the strings, watch them race. My younger brother innovates with headlines he tears from the Press-Citizen: *Local Boy Bowls 7-10 Split!* Up, up it goes. The rogue German Shepherd is trying to bite everyone. *Couple Wed 75 Years Die Fifteen Minutes Apart.* Heavenward. O glorious day! The kites bob and weave, boxed by the wind. The German Shepherd runs in circles. *Planets Collide!*

Bill comes hopping out of the barn screaming. His knee wide open, dangling, meat falling off the bone. The German Shepherd insane over the blood. They'd been jumping from the hayloft, Bill and the girlfriend, his knee sliced by something under the straw. Some farm implement lying in wait. Some menacing blade. *Space Aliens Take Over House of Representatives!* To the clouds! Bill, howling. Blood just everywhere. His knee inside the German Shepherd's jaws.

Nobody sees Uncle John until he's there, taking aim. A blast. Bill on the ground alive and bleeding. The German Shepherd dead. Little brother still tearing up the newspaper. *Rickety Kites Survive Nuclear Blast!* The kites, untethered, rise higher and disappear. Our faces upturned like prayer.

Loose Canon

He has a loose ponytail, hair strands falling without apparent purpose yet indefinite gravity. He nods while listening to stay grounded, so that his ballooned head full of trivia doesn't get stuck on the capital of South Dakota (Pierre) or how India is exactly 11 ½ hours ahead of Chicago or that Fluffernutter has less than 1% of actual marshmallow... so that his head won't ascend. He hums sad songs that remind him why he is here, soaring among skyscrapers, turning most orbits around so they appear backwards.

He makes a list of what matters most, maneuvering around the doodled spirals on his page, trying to remember what he's already learned from that last self-help conference in Roswell, the one when he left after the first day, claiming it was all re-threads of useless information, except the notes he took when Sarah Palin, keynote speaker, led the morning in jingoistic jargon:

1) Say something surprising to a stranger every day, something in gibberish.

2) When you have an overnight visitor, (Bristol), don't leave out your old underwear, worn bathrobes, hand-cuffs, the unfinished *New York Times* crossword puzzles. Hide them in an upstairs closet.

3) What they don't know is I can see Russia with my eyes closed.

4) "I do not like this Uncle Sam. I do not like his health care scam. I do not like these dirty crooks, or how they lie and cook the books. I do not like when Congress steals, I do not like their crony deals."

5) Creating gun-free zone schools is "stupid on steroids."

6) Polls are for strippers and cross-country skiers.

Swell

He lived with a woman who sold balloons at the zoo. She came home nights smelling of animal musk, giraffe saliva, people sweat, and cotton candy. She was always tired. Keeping oneself planted to the earth while holding onto three dozen helium balloons was no small task. And she was a small woman. She barely reached to his shoulders when they danced, had to glide along on the tops of his feet like a child.

Business was not exactly booming.

You should dress as a clown, he said.

Nooo. They would expect me to be funny.

It was true she wasn't funny. She had a calm, somewhat grave temperament, a formal manner with adults and children alike. Once she told him, *I see no reason to treat children differently. They prefer you to treat them with respect. They don't mind you spelling things out, like sorry kid, there are no Pikachu balloons and there never will be. A kid can deal with that. It's the parents who are pussies.*

In an attempt to strengthen her balloon-holding hand, she purchased a Captains of Crush hand-gripper from Amazon, and squeezed it in the evenings as they watched Cops. She was uninterested in rising into the heavens.

I could dress as a clown and accompany you, he said. *Be your sidekick.* Their relationship was fractured. He'd decided they needed to spend more time together. Also, he was unemployed.

She agreed and he became the best clown in all the land, or at least the zoo. Soon he was making more money than she, from tips the people tossed as he rode a unicycle and honked a horn and told his corny jokes.

The children called him Yuck-Yuck.

Her balloons began to wither and fade. Despair settled on her tiny shoulders like so much elephant dander. At night, his wig and rubber nose cast aside, he sat at the kitchen table counting the day's haul as she puttered around fixing sandwiches, making tea.

She plunked down his cup. Some of the hot tea sloshed onto the dollar bills he'd carefully smoothed and stacked.

I should quit, he said.

No way. You're super amazing at clowning. It's like you were born to it.

He'd read somewhere that 75% of all compliments were sarcastic.

I love you, he said. *I love you more than clowning. I love you more than all of this money.* He tossed the bills into the air like confetti. It was all an act though. He really loved clowning and he really loved money and she was beginning to get on his nerves.

She sat cross-legged on the floor, scooping up the cash, and putting it in her mouth, chewing, swallowing. Gagging a little.

There's nothing filthier than money, he said. *You're swelling up.*

She stuffed dollar bill after dollar bill into her face, which was now the size of a basketball. She stopped momentarily to smile at him. Really smile at him. Maybe she would die. She stuffed another handful into her mouth. He made no attempt to stop her.

A Box

"We don't have to live in a rectangular box," Van says. "We could move to the country, someplace like Alabama."

"Are you serious?" I ask. It's the first thing he's said after waking this morning. "They'd string us up there. Our kind."

We're inside our refrigerator box, the sun presses through the cracks already making me sweat.

Van stretches out, his six-foot frame nearly reaches both ends of the box. "I think we'll have some challenges when the snow flies."

I know he's right, he always is. But Alabama? Just the thought of it makes me grimace.

"What about that half built house on Victor Road? We could sleep in the basement, then vanish before the workers arrive every morning." I sit up, rub my eyes, hear a wasp dive-bombing, perhaps curious what is inside. Food? Bzzz. Shelter? Bzzz.

Van lies back, hands behind his head. Stares up at the minute cracks in the box. Sometimes the cardboard smell nauseates me. Like rotting ramen noodles. "I like it here. Nobody else to deal with. It's like we're invisible."

That was the part of this life that appealed to me too. Hiding out, like burrowing into a cave, or underground. "Yes, I agree."

"Plus, that house is so exposed. No trees close by, no wind. Welcome to suburbia."

"True." I nod. I know because I grew up in that house, before they demolished it.

Collection Day

One day in a small town outside Portland, the people rose from their beds and began throwing away all their possessions. It was Tuesday. The garbage trucks would not come until Wednesday, but they moved as if responding to orders barked from a megaphone.

Todd Blankenship marched out of his house with a desk lamp in each hand and several baseball caps stacked on his head. He pitched the lamps to the curb and bowed, the caps cascading into a pile. He gave Mrs. Ter Beest an airy high five as she tossed nine perfectly fine umbrellas onto her own curb. Her boy, Matty, pedaled his Big Wheel down the driveway, got off, and with a hard kick sent it careening past the piles of castoffs into the middle of the street.

He looked at his mother. "Leave it," she said.

Old man Chutney came out again and again with boxes of food. The perishables: mounds of ground beef, a salmon filet, pale chicken breasts wrapped in plastic. A sixteen-ounce carton of large curd cottage cheese. (He loved cottage cheese.) The dry goods: a box of angel hair spaghetti, cans of Campbell's Bean with Bacon soup, a large tin of Maxwell House coffee.

There was little eye contact and nobody spoke, though Ms. Felcher, the kindergarten teacher, hummed a song she'd taught her students, something about working hard every day with a smile, smile, smile. And she was smiling as she hummed and dragged her mattress out, then the plastic Santa climbing out of a plastic chimney, the Minnesota Vikings jersey that belonged to her ex-boyfriend that she slept in sometimes, a package of disposable nail files, the coasters with depictions of Civil War scenes her grandfather had given her.

She hesitated over the battery-operated waterfall, but added that to the pile, too.

By late afternoon, the streets smelled of sweat and dust, of machinery and old books and sour milk. The only sounds were the odd ringtones from discarded cell phones, the screeching of crows jostling for scraps.

The streets clogged with Hefty bags and furniture and clothes and food and art. Bicycles and lawnmowers and bottles of shampoo and toys. The people all stood on the grass, at a loss, as the sun began to droop.

Then, as if a whistle had been blown, they began to shed their clothes. Bermuda shorts and sundresses and Levis and Nikes were thrown to the piles. Even the babies were stripped of their onesies and their sailor dresses and their Pampers. Old Man Chutney undressed down to his socks, which he refused to remove.

A beaming moon rose and propelled them off their lawns into the clotted streets. The naked women and men and teenagers and toddlers and babies glowed like rich people's teeth as they threw themselves upon the piles of their worldly belongings. And there they lay, tangled and weary, waiting for collection.

The Guy in This Sky

The last time I saw a night sky like this he was smothering me, grinding his hips against mine, gnashing lips, and grunting like a feral pig. I kept stealing glimpses at the clouds, and certain shapes I could still make out, divisions in the transitioning sky: Yogi Bear and a headless Boo Boo were over his left shoulder, and if I squinted just right, up past my big toe, Marilyn Manson floated on the horizon.

I have no idea where he ended up after his stint in the state pen. Somebody told me he ditched the wife and kids and took off to the Bay Area. But I couldn't picture a redneck living among all those tree huggers and granola eaters. Nah, I'll bet he headed for some deader place like Alaska. A place too cold for even the fuzz to find you. A place where you sleep with a gun under your pillow.

I'd been cleaning this old lady's house in Webster. It

was his idea to knock her out, and case the place. Went south when the laced tea didn't work. The pillow sure did, or so the papers said. I fled, never returned home. Ran like an antelope, hid out in Penny's cellar. Became a mole.

And occasionally, on nights like this one, I wander out to that back pasture, and roll around in the long grass. I can hear the sounds of barreling horse hooves, and the first cut hay in Dinty's fields wafts by. And the groans emerge from somewhere deep inside me, as the light fades, and the night sky paints a song so familiar that I have to bury my head.

A Proper Party

Sadie stands at the kitchen counter assembling hors d'oeuvres for her daughter's graduation party. She slathers peanut butter into the canals of the celery sticks, positions raisins on top. She makes maybe forty-five of these until it occurs to her that she may have enough. She watches the little TV and tries to think of what other foods her daughter liked. The county is under a tornado watch until 6:00 p.m.

Her brother and his husband, Norm, walk in, holding bunches of balloons. The balloons are black with CONGRATS GRAD on them in gold.

"What a great idea," Sadie says, as they release the balloons and allow them to roam free. "I'm making food."

Her brother says, "I could use a drink." So she pours both him and Norm good, strong gin and tonics.

Norm opens the sliding door and steps out onto the deck. "The sky's green," he says.

"Tornado watch. Hold on, they've upgraded it to a warning," Sadie says.

She wonders how many will show up. A few had called to say they couldn't come but that they would be thinking of her.

Her brother sits on the stool at the counter and slurps his drink. "Can I help with anything?"

"Do you think fish sticks are a weird thing to serve at a party? Fish sticks and salsa?"

"Yes. Definitely."

A gust of cold wind blows through the house. The balloons mingle and dance. A small vase of daisies topples and spills over the counter. Breathing heavily, Sadie hustles about closing windows. Her brother cleans up the daisies as Norm comes back in shivering.

"Oh my," Sadie says. "Now what?" She wanders into the family room and sits on the sofa. She has made a display on the mantel there. Photographs, her daughter's awards, a drawing of a cat and a rooster from the third grade. Her brother and Norm follow and sit on either side of her. The tornado sirens wail.

"I love that sound," Norm says. He takes Sadie's hand. "We should go down to the basement."

"He's right dear," her brother says. Nobody moves. The windows judder.

"But I made a cake," she says.

"We can celebrate another time. We can celebrate any time we want," her brother says. "You know she wouldn't mind."

The balloons skirt along the ceiling, their strings dangling. Sadie stands and gathers a few of them.

"We can take these down to the basement. I have a radio down there. You two can carry the food."

It's an old house and the basement has a cement floor and some boxes of old things, the daughter's things, and not much else. The lights flicker and Norm lights some candles just before the power goes out completely. Outside they hear a roaring sound. Sadie's worried about the batteries in the radio but they turn it on and it works. Her brother tunes in to the local station but it's just the Emergency Broadcast System and not the cool jazz they were hoping for, so he switches it off again.

"We could sing," Sadie says. The roaring gets louder.

"Come here," her brother says. They sit on the floor together and he wraps her in his arms. Norm kneels and wraps his arms around them both.

The tornado sounds like an approaching locomotive. Upstairs, crashing, a window breaking.

"I wanted a proper party," Sadie says.

Her brother and his husband squeeze her tight.

Now, stillness. The balloons settle into their places, the candles burn steadily. Sadie's brother wants to go upstairs and check the damage, but she says, "No, I'm not ready yet." So they eat the celery and the fish sticks. And when they finish, they cut the cake and eat that, too.

No Soul

She had mastered the art of looking aloof.

"Look, I'm sorry I broke your snow bong," I said.

"What were you thinking?" she asked.

"I wanted to try it with absinthe instead of snow. Can't blame me for experimenting."

We were driving to the shooting gallery. Tamra almost refused to go after I accidentally broke the German exchange student's nose last weekend. We were partying on Bear Hill. He was a little too cozy, a little too suggestive. I called him a tea snob and he took a swing. Missed.

"I'm worried about your level of aggression," Tamra said. She rolled her window halfway down.

It wasn't the first time I'd punched someone in the face, so I said nothing. Last time I ended up worse. He was over a foot taller. Oops.

"You shouldn't be smoking pot, anyhow," I said. "Bake some brownies."

She glared at me, her ginger hair flying in every direction. "When you eat it, it's different."

I've never eaten pot. It's too expensive. Crack is cheaper than pot, but then, so is candy.

We pulled in the driveway of the gallery. I turned off the car. The security guard loomed by the entrance. There was a new sign over the doors: Lookaws.

"What the hell is that supposed to mean?" Tamra said.

"No clue." I shrugged, fished my Browning Citori Skeet Gun out of the back of my truck. "Maybe a mistake."

"I don't give a shit about typos," Tamra said, "But it's a little weird. I mean, what kind of legit business would hang a dumbass sign that doesn't mean anything?"

She had a point. Still, I was looking forward to shooting.

This Is How Eventually the World Falls Apart

Your brother wears his school uniform, the black slacks, the white oxford shirt and red tie, every day of the summer holiday. He buys an afro wig and a pair of glasses at Busby-Wing Drug. He wants to look like Malcolm X, though he is white and thirteen years old and doesn't know much about him. After a few weeks, grime paints his collar and the knees of his black trousers go shiny with wear. Your mother refuses to wash the uniform, thinking this will somehow discourage the behavior. She buys him a baseball mitt and sets it on his pillow, but he simply hangs the mitt on his doorknob and never looks at it again. *Your father and I are so glad you don't give us any trouble,* your mother tells you, but you'd like a wig of your own. Your brother preaches to you and the neighbor kids from his pulpit in the garage. *This is a time of great upheaval.* You believe him. You believe *in* him. One morning he irons the shirt himself, standing in his boxer shorts in a cloud of steam. When the steam saturates the sweat of his shirt and the smell worms itself through the rooms like the green death in *The Ten Commandments*, your dad lays down his newspaper, says, *This is exactly what I'm talking about.*

Dream Maker

Charlotte shakes the powdered snow from her head while she stuffs the last bite, a large portion of her coffeecake muffin, into her eager mouth.

"Wow," is all you can say.

When she finishes chewing, and swallowing her HOT morsel, face flushes, she turns to you and says, "Blow me."

And for a handmade moment, an ever-ready slice of brute force wind nearly sends you far flung.

"Also," Charlotte adds, "my brothers are both here. Corner table." She nods. "They could notch the fucking daylights out of you."

You baffle-think: *I'm just a traveler on this highway,* while you touch her arm, ask random questions about Uruguay. Possible probates. Fiscal cliffs.

She murmurs, "Imagine this: a universal space in which you choose one precipitation. Only one. And it never changes."

You smile, already drenched in acid rain. Dancing. Arms akimbo, you blanch toward the road, a whirling dervish.

Akimbo

We're painting the nursery in the nude. Slapping eggshell over walls the color of a baby's tongue. We've been at it awhile. The pink keeps bleeding through. We're not using drop cloths because the carpet's getting ripped up anyway—this sort of sculpted wall-to-wall that reminds me of my grandmother's house and smells like cigarettes and corn. So we're manic about it, spattering ourselves, our glasses, our hair and forearms, our privates. You paint a heart on your chest. I smear a swath across my forehead. A Flock of Seagulls song plays on the radio. There's a tremor and it makes us stop. Now a jolt and you go, *Whoa Nellie.* The windowglass trembles. Bits of plaster copter to the floor. Paint sloshes out of the can. You're trying to reach me and all I can think of is the electric football game me and my brothers had when we were kids and how we'd work forever setting up our offensive and defensive lines and when we'd finally flip the switch, all the little plastic players just stood in one place and vibrated impotently. This is you now, beautiful and vibrating, your arms akimbo, looking like all you want is to break free, achieve forward momentum, catch me, before the world splits apart.

Acknowledgments / Kathy Fish

Thank you to the editors of the following journals where these stories have appeared or will appear: "Abandon All Thoughts" in *The Journal of Compressed Creative Arts*; "Endangered ~ Out of Place ~ A Botched Affair" in *Heavy Feather Review*; "Woe" in *Harpoon Review*; "Grip" in *RKVRY*; "The Four O'Clock Bird" in *People Holding*; "River" in *Vignette Review*; "We Learned to Pronounce Prokofiev" in *Change Seven Magazine*; "The Possibility of Bears" in *Keyhole Magazine*; "Vocabulary" and "Bear" in *Gone Lawn*; "Pulse," "Swell," and "No Time for Prairie Dog Town" in *FRiGG*; "Enigma," "Game Show," and "Peacock" in *Wigleaf;* "Tool" in *Corium Magazine*; "Love Train ~ Lifelike ~ Spill," "A Pirate Or A Cowboy," and "Neal Figgens," in *Connotation Press*; "Strings" in *New World Writing*; "Go Dog" in *Sundog Lit;* "The Blue of Milk" in *Blue Fifth Review*; "Come Loose and Fly Away" in *Salon Zine*; "Akimbo" in *Stripped* (Lulu, 2011); "A Room With Many Small Beds" in *Threadcount;* "Hello" and "A Proper Party" in *Revolution John*; "This Is How Eventually the World Falls Apart" in *Slice Magazine*; "Sea Creatures of Indiana" forthcoming in *Alice Blue*; "Collection Day" in *New South*; and "Düsseldorf" forthcoming in *Yemassee Journal*.

Acknowledgments/ Robert Vaughan

"The Rooms We Rented" in *Doctor T.J. Eckleberg Review*; "She Wears Me Like A Coat" in *Santa Fe Literary Review*; "Last Exit From Liberty" in *Entropy*; "Night Life" in *LA Weekly*; "Temporary" in *The Brooklyner*; "Figurines" in *Flash Fiction Fridays*; "Fling" in *Camroc Press Review*; "Rejection" in *50 to 1*; "When He Left it all to Me" in *The Miscreant*; "Help, I'm Alive" in *Festival of Language*; "Pets: Three Vignettes" in *Revolution John*; "Postcards of a Life" in *Postcard Shorts*; "Dew Drop Inn" in *52/250*; "Dehydration" in *Elimae*; "Keep it Curt" in *Rabbit Hole*; "Four Stone Cups" (originally "Abdul") in *Indigo Rising*; "Picnic" in *Eunoia Review*; "No Face World Champ" in *theNewerYork*; "Too Much Oxygen" in *Literary Orphans*; "A Box" in *Connotation Press*; "The Guy in This Sky" in *Metazen*; "Dream Maker" in *Thrice Magazine*.

"The Rooms We Rented" was a finalist for the Gertrude Stein Award in 2014.

Kathy Fish has joined the faculty of the Mile-High MFA at Regis University in Denver. She will be teaching flash fiction. Additionally, she teaches two-week intensive Fast Flash© Workshops. Recently, she served as Consulting Editor for the Queen's Ferry Press *The Best Small Fictions 2015*. *Rift*, co-authored with Robert Vaughan, is her fourth collection.

Her stories have been published or are forthcoming in *The Lineup: 20 Provocative Women Writers* (Black Lawrence Press, 2015), *Choose Wisely: 35 Women Up to No Good* (Upper Rubber Boot Books, 2015), *Slice, Guernica, Indiana Review, Mississippi Review* online, *Denver Quarterly, New South, Yemassee Journal* and various other journals and anthologies. She was the guest editor of Dzanc Books' *Best of the Web 2010*. She is the author of three collections of short fiction: a chapbook of flash fiction in the chapbook collective, *A Peculiar Feeling of Restlessness: Four Chapbooks of Short Short Fiction by Four Women* (Rose Metal Press, 2008), *Wild Life* (Matter Press, 2011) and *Together We Can Bury It* (The Lit Pub, 2012).

www.kathyfish.com

Robert Vaughan leads roundtables at Red Oak Writing in Milwaukee, WI. He also teaches workshops in hybrid writing, dialogue, playwriting at places like The Clearing in Door County, WI. He was the co-founder of Flash Fiction Fridays, a radio program on WUWM in Milwaukee, where he premiered local flash fiction writers, and also starred writers from America and abroad. He is a senior editor for JMWW, and Lost in Thought magazines, a guest editor for Uno Kudo #5. Rift, co-authored with Kathy Fish, is his fourth collection.

His writing has been published in over 500 various literary journals, such as *Necessary Fiction, Elimae, Literary Orphans, Everyday Genius, The Lit Pub,* and *Nervous Breakdown.* He's also been selected for many anthologies such as *Stripped* (2012), *Flash Fiction Funny* (2014), and *This is Poetry* (2015). He is the author of three collections: *Microtones* (Cervena Barva Press, 2012); *Diptychs + Triptychs + Lipsticks + Dipshits* (Deadly Chaps, 2013); and *Addicts & Basements* (CCM, 2014). He also edited *Flash Fiction Fridays* (2011). His awards include Micro-Fiction (2012), Gertrude Stein Awards (2013, 2014) and a Professional of the Year Award from Strathmore's Who's Who for outstanding contributions and achievements as an author (2015).

www.robert-vaughan.com

CPSIA information can be obtained at www.ICGtesting.com
Printed in the USA
BVOW08s0617050116

431691BV00003BA/59/P

9 780996 352604